Lewis & Clark
AND
Davey Hutchins

To Melissa

[signature]

Lewis & Clark
AND
Davey Hutchins

by Nolan Carlson
Illustrated by Becky Bryant

Hearth

PUBLISHING

HILLSBORO, KANSAS

Lewis & Clark and Davey Hutchins
Copyright ©1994 by Hearth Publishing

Second Edition
Printed in the USA
by Mennonite Press, Inc.

Cover Illustration: Becky Bryant
Story Illustrations: Becky Bryant

Publisher's Cataloging in Publication
(Prepared by Quality Books Inc.)

Carlson, Nolan K.
    Lewis and Clark and Davey Hutchins / Nolan K. Carlson.
    p. cm.
    SUMMARY: A novel about the Lewis and Clark expedition, as seen through the eyes of a thirteen-year-old boy, Davey Hutchins.
    Preassigned LCCN: 93-80993.
    ISBN 1-882420-08-X

    1. Explorers—Juvenile fiction. 2. Lewis and Clark Expedition—(1804-1806)—Juvenile fiction. I. Title.

PZ7.C3757Le 1994   [Fic]
                                            QBI94-142

To Lorena and the grandkids,
Zac and Chelsey

LEWIS AND CLARK AND DAVEY HUTCHINS
Chapter 1

"Don't die, Pa! Please, don't die!" I remembered shouting those words just hours before.

Leaning against a tree behind the cabin, I choked back my tears. I told myself I was too old to cry like a baby, but I couldn't deny the hurt I felt. The stars twinkled in a cloudless sky. Everything seemed the same, normal. But, it wasn't the same; my Pa had died today.

Uncle Abner draped his arm around my shoulders and squeezed me hard. I continued to stare into the woods. I breathed in Uncle Abner's pipe tobacco. His breath and his clothes gave it off.

"He went easy, Davey, boy," Uncle Abner said.

Words lodged in my throat. All I could do was nod my head in agreement.

"A better man never lived than your Pa," he said. "I think after your Ma died, Davey, he started dying a little too."

Self-consciously, I muffed at my tear-filled eyes and looked away.

"That pneumonia is a treacherous thing."

"I thought Doc Greenwood would save him," I said. "I brought him clear from St. Louis. Maybe if I had hurried faster Pa would be alive."

"St. Louis is a mighty long way off, Davey. The fastest coach and horse in the world couldn't have made it quicker than three days. You got back in less time than that."

Uncle Abner released my shoulder. "No. There was nothing that could be done. Your Pa was a very sick man."

Sounds of the forest filled the night around us. Crickets and locusts chirped and an owl hooted mournfully in the distance. Jake, my pet crow, flew to my shoulder. I shivered, pulling my jacket tighter around me. Even though the night was warm, I felt chilled.

Uncle Abner turned and looked down at me. Standing there, I thought he seemed as tall and sturdy as a tree. He cleared his throat uneasily. "You'll come back with us after the burial, of course. Your Aunt Maude and I would be proud to have you. We've never been blessed with children." He shifted his feet. "Of course, I know we could never take the place of your beloved parents, but we'd give you a good home."

I squinted at a star all blurred from the tears in my eyes.

"We'd enroll you in school. You could learn to read and write."

"Pa already taught me how to read and write," I said stubbornly.

"But school would be different. You'd learn about our American history and about other countries. I've heard claims that because of a huge land purchase from France we've doubled the size of this country. There's talk that there's plans right now to start exploring this new region." He shook his head. "Why, I hear that there are places where people are the color of copper and have idols of solid gold. There are places where huge snow-capped mountains stick up into the clouds and places where the water's so deep you'd never touch bottom."

"I don't need any of those places," I said looking away. "All I need is right here — this farm." I put my arms out and gestured. Jake fluttered his wings.

"You do have a right nice farm here, Davey. But, you can't run it by yourself now that your Pa's gone."

I turned in defiance, my hands knotted into tight balls. "And why can't I? I'm old enough. Pa was on his own at my age. He and I cleared the land together. We planted and took care of it. I've plowed behind the mule for hours at a time. I know every inch of this farm."

2

"But there's not a living soul for twenty miles. What if you'd get sick or hurt, God forbid?"

I rubbed my boot along my dog's back lying at my feet. He looked up with sad eyes. "Snooker will be with me," I said proudly. "If something happened, he would fetch someone."

"Snooker's a mighty fine dog, Davey. But, he's not human." Uncle Abner shook his head. "No. I'd never forgive myself if I didn't take care of you proper-like."

Turning, I grabbed the pocket on Uncle Abner's vest. "But, Uncle Abner, sir...I was born here. I haven't been to town over a half dozen times in my entire life. And the times I did go I hated it. There were so many people milling around. Horses, carts, wagons, and carriages crowded the streets. The smell of garbage made me sick."

"You'd get used to it, Davey," he argued. "Besides, it's not all that way. Why, your Aunt Maude and I have a nice house with a big backyard."

"The whole forest is my backyard," I muttered.

"There'd be a whole lot of new people for you to get to know. Just across the street there's some nice boys and girls your age."

"I don't want to meet any new kids." I shook my head. "I've got Snooker and the animals in the woods. Deer come up and eat out of my hand. Squirrels and crows perch on my shoulder. They're better than any humans."

"But, you need to be around people."

"Preacher Popkus comes around once every other month and reads Bible verses and prays with us. He's the only human I need. He'll help me with my soul."

"Someday you could take over my store if you learn the trade well."

I shook my head. "I'm a farmer and I'll always be a farmer."

Uncle Abner sighed, walked over to me, and put his arm around my shoulder again. "I understand how you

3

feel, Davey, boy. Your Ma died and now your Pa." He looked skyward. "I suppose He, in His wisdom, has a plan. Your parents are gone and now here we are trying to pull you away from the place you love most, your home."

With one awkward movement I turned to the big, kind-hearted man and buried my face in the coarse wool of his vest. The sorrow bubbled through me and I heard the cries of pain fly from my mouth into the night. It didn't sound like me. It was scratchy and high-pitched.

Uncle Abner stood there, his hand tapping easily on my back, and let me drain myself of the hurt that had been bottled up. I was grateful to him. He was much like Pa, I thought.

After a time I stepped back and wiped my nose. The pains in my belly and chest were gone. Uncle Abner handed me a handkerchief and I blew my nose with a loud honk.

"Maybe a little supper now and a good night's sleep is what's in order."

I nodded but said nothing.

"I think your Aunt Maude is cooking something real tasty in the cabin. What say you and I go see what it is?"

"I guess I am a little hungry," I said pulling on my hat. I nudged Snooker with my toe. He looked up and his ears stood straight on end. "Want something to eat, old boy?" I asked looking down at him through the darkness. Snooker whimpered and his tail started to rock back and forth.

"Davey, let's not talk about you coming to live with us or anything until after the burial," Uncle Abner said. "Would that be all right with you, lad?"

"Yes, sir," I said. "That'd be all right."

Uncle Abner and I walked back together toward the cabin with Snooker close at our heels. The smell of home-made bread leaked out of the cabin windows and I felt ashamed for feeling hungry.

4

Chapter 2

I forced myself to concentrate on what the schoolmaster was saying. Soon my mind floated out the window. I saw the schoolmaster's mouth open and close and the flap of skin jiggle up and down on his throat, but I wasn't thinking of what he was saying. My mind was outside running with Snooker. I saw him lying in a spot of packed dirt beneath that big tree in the schoolyard waiting for the end of the day. When Master Boggs rang the bell old Snooker would jump to his feet, his ears straight up, and wait for the kids to come flying out the door.

I thought back over the last three months in St. Louis. I did love Aunt Maude and Uncle Abner; they had been very kind to me. Aunt Maude tried her best to "civilize" me with store bought shoes and clothes. She showed me the proper way to eat at the table and how to greet her friends passing by the house. She took me regularly to church and poked me with her elbow when my thoughts strayed from the preacher's words.

They did have a big backyard, but it was nothing compared to the wilderness back home. Uncle Abner took me out to the country on Sunday afternoons and let me swim in the creek. He spent hours teaching me the mercantile trade. Uncle Abner even let me "try" his pipe. I coughed until I turned red as clay. He made me promise on my life never to tell Aunt Maude about it.

I thought back to my years on the farm and I had a hard time to keep from bawling. It almost seemed like a dream to me now. Someone else was living in our cabin. Someone else was plowing and planting our fields. The cows, chickens, mules, and land had been sold. The thing that really hurt was the thought of leaving Ma and Pa there, side by side, in the ground now owned by strangers.

I howled, feeling the sharp sting of a hickory stick strike my knuckles.

"David Hutchins, are you so smart that you don't have to listen to today's lesson?"

Master Boggs stared down at me. His little gray eyes were almost closed behind his square spectacles. I tried not to look at the flap of skin jiggling at his throat.

"Yes...yes, sir," I said stammering. "I mean, no, sir. I'm not that smart."

"Well, Mr. Hutchins admits that there are areas in which his education is lacking." He turned and smiled smugly at the rest of the class.

My ears turned red hearing the giggles of the class.

"Mr. Hutchins, will you be so kind as to tell the class who Thomas Jefferson's Secretary of War is?"

I swallowed weakly. "No, sir." I scooted down on my bench.

"Can you tell me who the Secretary of State is?"

"No, sir." I was sure my ears were smoking.

Master Boggs leaned down and grinned. His gold tooth reflected the sun. "So, you haven't heard a word I said. You know nothing about our government. You know nothing about President Jefferson's Cabinet. You know nothing about the biggest land purchase in history."

I sat straight up in my seat. "But I do, Master Boggs. I do know about it!" I shouted.

The schoolmaster placed a finger to his lips in thought. "You do know who the Secretary of War and the Secretary of State are?"

I shook my head. "No, not that. But, I do know about the big land purchase. I've been following it in the papers for months. My Uncle Abner and I talk about it all of the time."

Master Boggs gazed about the classroom with a surprised look on his face. "For three months you've hardly opened your mouth. You've shown no interest in any of our lessons. Suddenly, you are full of information." He nodded and his spectacles slid to the tip of his nose. "Suppose you tell us about the biggest land purchase in history."

Slowly, I got to my feet and cleared my throat. For the first time since entering school in St. Louis, I felt confident. Master Boggs stepped back and every eye was on me.

"Well," I said, "the land was purchased from France on May 2, 1803 for $15,000,000. Our government purchased over a million square miles for about four cents an acre. Mr. Monroe and Mr. Livingston represented the United States in the deal. Mr. Talleyrand represented France." I smiled to myself watching the students sit forward on their benches with interest. "Some men think that there's a northwestern water passage from the Atlantic to the Pacific Ocean through this new territory. No one really knows what's out there but some Indians tell of huge mountains to the west. The exciting thing is the exploring of this new land. Two men are taking command of the expedition at Jefferson's request. They are Merriweather Lewis from Virginia, a captain in the army, and William Clark his good friend from Kentucky. In fact," I said with pride, "Clark is right here in St. Louis waiting for Lewis to join him. Uncle Abner said they'll leave in a few days from St. Charles once they have all of their men and supplies." I took a breath and prepared to continue.

Master Boggs raised his hand. "That'll be enough, Hutchins. I think you've convinced me and the class that you do know about this new land purchase." A twinkle appeared in his little eyes. "But, you still don't know about our President's Cabinet."

A bony finger poked beneath my nose.

"The Secretary of State is James Madison and the Secretary of War is Henry Dearborn."

Master Boggs cleared his throat and I lowered myself back to my bench. "I would like you to write those facts five hundred times so it'll sink into that "bumpkin" head of yours."

I felt sick as I gazed at the sneers and smiles on the faces around the room. There was only one person who was not smiling, Priscilla James. She was perhaps the most beautiful girl in the world. Her reddish-gold curls fell down to her shoulders. Her complexion was as smooth as cream. She had the tiniest waist and the prettiest dimples. At this moment she had a look of sympathy on her face. For a second our eyes met and I felt a warm glow of embarrassment creep up the back of my neck. Prissy, as all the kids and even Master Boggs called her, looked shyly away. I was sure I saw a hint of a blush on her cheeks.

Angrily, I grabbed my paper. Running a finger around my stiff collar, I started on the schoolmaster's instructions. My mouth silently led my fingers as I wrote the first of the five hundred sentences. 'The Secretary of State is James Madison and the Secretary of War is Henry Dear...' I looked up catching Prissy looking at me out of the corner of her eye.

Master Boggs searched the paper trying to find an error in the five hundred sentences. The sun had lowered and I knew Aunt Maude would be wondering what kept me. I also knew that when I explained what happened I would "catch it" from her. This would never have happened if I had stayed on the farm. Out there, a fellow didn't have to know anything about a President's Cabinet. If you knew how to plant, take care of livestock, and use your hands that was all that was necessary.

"Ahemmm...Mister Hutchins..." Master Boggs looked over his little spectacles. "I find nothing wrong with these sentences, so you may leave now."

I jumped to my feet and started down the aisle toward the door.

"Hutchins!"

I froze in my tracks.

"You have not been excused yet, young man," the schoolmaster said, his voice shrill.

Turning, I tried to look sorry. "I'm sorry, Master Boggs. May I please be excused now?" I asked.

The schoolmaster paused for a moment and then nodded. "You may leave. Just remember the proper way to excuse yourself from my school room."

"Yes, sir, I will," I said softly. ("You skinny, crosseyed, stupid donkey,") I said under my breath all the time smiling pleasantly at him.

Master Boggs dismissed me with a wave of his hand and I walked at a fast pace out the door and down the stone steps of the school.

My eyes searched for Snooker waiting for me. Prissy James was sitting beside Snooker patting him about the muzzle and head.

I had a wild urge to turn and run but my feet wouldn't obey. Slowly, I scuffed toward her, my heart beating like a drum.

Prissy looked up and smiled. My knees went weak.

"Hello," she said. "I saw your dog lying here waiting for you. I thought I'd keep him company. I hope you don't mind."

"No...no, that's okay." I bit my tongue.

Prissy patted a spot beside her. "Sit down with us."

I couldn't believe my good luck. Before today I didn't think Prissy James knew I was alive."

"I love Snooker," she said. She ran her hand along his muzzle. "He's so gentle."

I sat down crosslegged beside her. "Don't...don't you have a dog?"

Prissy looked sad. I knew I had brought up a bad subject.

"Well, you see, my dog Misty, got run over by a lumber-wagon a few months ago." She sighed. "I miss her."

"I'm...I'm sorry to hear that," I said, wanting to do something to comfort her.

Her face brightened. "I've watched Snooker waiting out here every day for you. He must really love you."

"I guess he does. But, it couldn't be half as much as I love him," I said, and then regretted it. I thought it sounded too syrupy.

"Someday, father will get me a new dog." She shook her head and the curls floated in the wind. "But, right now I don't want a new one. Not until the hurt of Misty is gone."

I swallowed. "I can understand that. I'd feel the same way if anything happened to Snooker."

She shrugged. "I've watched you a lot since you came to school three months ago."

My face started turning red. "Why?"

Prissy played with one of her curls winding it slowly around her finger.

Snooker looked at one and then the other as we spoke.

"I noticed something different about you, that's all."

I glanced away sure that my face was on fire.

"I mean, the other boys are such ninnys. All they think about is pulling a prank on someone. I think everyone, including Master Boggs, has treated you very badly." Her face became rosy with anger. "And I think today was the worst," she huffed. "I thought it was wonderful how much you knew about the big land purchase. Gracious, you knew more than I did and I'd wager you knew a whole lot more than the rest of the class, Master Boggs included."

I struggled to think of something to say. Finally, I simply said, "Thank you."

"I wanted you to know that you've got at least two friends here in St. Louis."

"Two?" I asked.

"Yes, silly; Snooker and me." She laughed.

I laughed with her. I thought I was going to float right

off the ground.

"I'm going to tell you a secret if you promise that you'll never tell," she said quietly.

I exed my heart and put up my hand. "I promise."

"I've been waiting out here for over an hour so I'd get to talk to you. Do you think that's silly?"

"No, I don't think that's silly." I patted Snooker. "I know Snooker liked the company."

Prissy threw her head back and laughed. She tapped me on the arm. I looked down at my arm vowing never to wash that spot the rest of my life.

"You were a farmer before you came to the city, weren't you, Davey?"

Nodding, I ran my hand down Snooker's haunch. "Yes, I was. My Pa and I had a farm about a hundred miles west of St. Louis. We grew corn, wheat, tobacco, and all of the vegetables we needed. We had three cows, two mules, and over thirty chickens." My chest swelled with pride.

Prissy smiled and looked impressed. "My, that was quite a farm."

"Yes, we farmed almost ten acres. Someday it would've been mine. I promised I'd never leave it." I lowered my eyes sadly.

Prissy reached out and touched my hand. "You look so sad."

I looked down, not believing my eyes. Her dainty hand was laying on my dark, sunburned hand. "It's sold to strangers. My Ma and Pa are buried there."

"I wish there was something I could do."

I shook my head. "I'm not a city boy and I never will be. I belong on the farm close to the wilderness where I can hunt, fish, trap, and work the soil."

"That sounds exciting! I would love to have seen your farm."

"I would like to show it to you." I shrugged. "Snooker and I don't fit here in the city."

"I'm sorry about that. Maybe after awhile you'll learn to adjust."

I shook my head. "I could live here fifty years and I still wouldn't like it. Uncle Abner is trying to make a store-keeper out of me. If I ever get the chance to leave, I'd take it in a minute."

Prissy looked away. "That'd mean we wouldn't see each other again. You wouldn't like that would you?"

Leaning forward, I shook my head. "Gosh, no. I wouldn't like that part. I think you're the prettiest girl I've ever seen."

Prissy looked down, her face glowing.

I clapped my hand over my mouth. "Gosh, I'm sorry. Aunt Maude would have a fit if she heard me talking this way."

She looked up and smiled. The glow was starting to fade from her cheeks. "It was a little forward. But, I liked hearing you say it." She giggled.

Relief flooded over me and I laughed with her.

"Well, I'd better go," she said smoothing her skirt. "I've got to meet father at the bank."

"Your father works at the bank?" I asked.

"He owns the bank. It's been in our family for years."

I gulped knowing that Prissy was from a very promi-nent St. Louis family. I should have guessed, I told myself. She was always dressed in the nicest clothes. Her man-ners were the very best. But, she never put on airs. Jumping to my feet, I helped her up.

Prissy took my hand. "Thank you, Davey," she said with a smile. "Just remember, no matter what happens you've got a friend."

"I'll remember that," I said.

With a toss of her curls, she turned and walked away.

I watched her until she was out of sight. At last, I sighed and looked down at Snooker still lying at my feet. "You know, old boy, St. Louis is not going to seem quite as bad as it used to seem."

Chapter 3

I felt guilty for playing hooky from school today, but I couldn't help myself. Ever since Uncle Abner told me last night that Lewis and Clark were staying at the Parker Hotel I couldn't get my mind off it. I waited all morning to get a glimpse of the famous explorers. Every time someone came out of the huge double doors of the Parker, I sat up straight wondering if that person was one of them. When the person attracted no attention, I slumped back to the ground with Snooker at my side.

Uncle Abner said Lewis wanted to sneak into town. He didn't want to waste time with a lot of fanfare. He wanted to meet with his friend Clark, order more supplies, obtain additional crew and be off.

I sat there, my eyes pasted to the doors, fondling one of Snooker's limp ears. People mingled around the hotel entrance for hours either waiting to catch a glimpse of the famous pair or hoping that they would be lucky enough to be one of those selected to go on the trek.

The doors swung open and I sat up. I jumped to my feet when I saw people starting to run and congregate around two men in front of the hotel. There were shouts and applause. People came from everywhere. Jumping up and down, I tried to see over the heads and shoulders of those blocking my view. Urgently, I got down on all fours and wiggled myself between peoples' legs to get a closer look. After getting my hat smashed flat and my fingers stepped on several times I found myself right in the middle of the inner circle so close to the explorers I could reach out and touch them.

At that moment, from this vantage point, they seemed bigger than life. They were both dressed in business suits

for they were in the process of buying and negotiating for the President and the United States Government. Both men were taller than the average man. Captain Lewis had a sober, business-like expression on his face. He seemed annoyed with all of the attention as though he had not a minute to waste on such matters. He had a sharp nose and chin. He was a young man not yet seeing his thirtieth birthday.

Lieutenant Clark was a few years older. I noticed his bright red hair blazing in the sunlight when he doffed his hat in greeting. He was a bit larger boned and heavier than Lewis. His blue eyes twinkled merrily as though he was having a wonderful time.

At last Captain Merriweather Lewis raised his hand for silence. He spoke: "Dear citizens of St. Louis, thank you for your warm welcome this morning. We would like very much to stop and chat with each and every one of you, but we are on an important mission for our President and our country and each moment of delay is critical." He turned and looked at Clark. "My friend and co-leader Lieutenant William Clark..."

Applause broke out for the well-liked Kentuckian.

Clark waved his hat and his ruddy face creased in a smile.

Captain Lewis continued. "...are leaving in just a few days from St. Charles on one of the most important and exciting ventures known to mankind. We are going to map, explore, and log the huge purchase of land from France. The acquisition of this land will double the size of our country. We have paused in Louisville and St. Louis to collect supplies and men for this journey. Supplies we can easily obtain, but men..." He paused and his bushy brows knitted together. "...must be strong and hearty and willing to withstand cold, hunger, Indians, and dangers we might not even be aware of. We want men who sincerely have a desire to see and be part of our country's destiny."

My heart hammered in my chest. I knew I was witnessing a great historical event.

Captain Lewis nodded to Lieutenant Clark. Clark held up his hand and smiled broadly. "I echo what Captain Lewis has just said. This trip will be a hard and treacherous one. It will be no Sunday picnic. But, I know that the hardy and adventurous men from Missouri will do us all proud."

The crowd responded to Clark with applause and cries of adoration.

"Our personnel officer, Sergeant Riley, will be interviewing men today and tomorrow right here in front of the Parker Hotel. We have already traveled from Louisville and will begin the trek in earnest from St. Charles in just a few days. We already have twenty men signed and need twenty-eight more. From the looks out there of some of you, I think we will fill our twenty-eight man quota quite easily." Again the congregation applauded. "Be prepared to be gone from your families and loved ones for many months. Be prepared to face hardships and death each and every day in the wilderness. If you have the will, courage, and desire for such a venture, stand in line and Sergeant Riley will take your name and interview you." He raised his hand once more and waved his hat. "And now, my friends of St. Louis, Captain Lewis and I have other urgent business, so please let us be on our way. Goodbye for now!" He waved once more and then, with Lewis, pushed through the crowd and entered a carriage to be transported to a government depot to line up needed supplies.

Sergeant Riley was instantly swarmed by men wanting to sign up for the trek. There was shouting, cursing, and pushing as men and youths fought for places in line.

I waited in the line only to be pushed back time and again. Snooker ran back and forth, his tail wagging frantically, barking with excitement. At times I was sure I was going to smother as I became lodged between burly

Missourians. Suddenly, I fell backwards as a shoving match started at the front of the line and sprawled me on the ground. Snooker rushed up and licked my face with concern. Men shouted and scattered forming a human circle for a wrestling match between two men vieing for the head of the line.

Looking up, I smiled seeing Sergeant Riley standing there craning his neck to get a view of the fight. No one was in line. I jumped to my feet, beat the dust from my breeches with my hat, and rushed to the head of the line.

"Sergeant Riley, sir...my name is Davey Hutchins and I'm here to sign up for the expedition," I said, looking up at the bearded face.

Sergeant Riley ignored me, his attention completely on the street ruckus.

I pulled at the fringes of the soldier's deerskin jacket. "Sergeant Riley, sir. I said I'm here to sign up for the expedition."

He looked down and spat. A slow, taunting smile came to his face. He spat once again and grinned revealing a row of teeth brown with tobacco stains. "Well, look what we have here," he said. "We've got a young pup wanting to do a man's job."

"I'm young, sir. But, I've lived in the wilderness all my life."

"And how many would that be, I'm wondering?" the sergeant asked in a graveled voice.

I paused, licking my lips. I crossed my fingers behind my back. "Eighteen, sir...yes, eighteen."

Sergeant Riley threw his head back and laughed. "You ain't any more eighteen than I am, young'un. There's not a sprig of hair on that smooth chin of yours."

My face got real hot. I nodded. "All right, maybe I'm not eighteen. But, I'm old enough to survive in the wilderness."

Sergeant Riley waved me away and returned his attention to the street fight. "Don't waste my time, lad. You're too young and that's all there is to it. We'll have enough to do without having to look after your welfare."

Reaching up, I pushed his shoulder again. "I'm not that old, but I'm strong and in real good health. I'm good with my hands. I can work twenty straight hours a day. I'm a crack shot and a good trapper. I could help put up and break camp. I could help pole the boat. I can handle any odd job that needs to be done. All I want is a chance."

He leaned down. He was so close I felt his warm breath on my face. His eyes squinted as he gestured with the pen in his hand. "See this?" He pointed to a red, puckered scar running diagnoally from the hair-line of his right temple, across the bridge of his nose, along his upper lip and then disappearing in his thick beard.

Looking at the deep, raw scar, I nodded.

"Well, my lad, an injun did that to me with a knife. He could have carved out both eyeballs if I hadn't moved quick. We'll likely meet with thousands of those with that same idea on their minds. They won't give no welcome. We're trespassing into the lands that they've lived on for centuries. Not a one of us may come back alive. We might all get an arrow or knife in the gut."

I swallowed.

The Sergeant smiled, revealing his bad teeth once more. "Now, you still want to go?"

"Yes, sir," I said without a blink of an eye.

"Get back!" the Sergeant ordered and shoved me hard. "Get back and let some men sign up here." He shoved me once more, his patience gone, and I flew to the ground.

Snooker sidled up next to me and licked the dirt from my face. Slowly, I got to my feet and started to shuffle home. Once, I looked back at the long line still waiting to sign up for the greatest venture known to mankind.

###

"A lot of excitement in town today, Davey," Uncle Abner said rattling a leaf of his newspaper.

I leaned closer to the fire and continued reading my history book.

"Lewis and Clark are about ready to take off for the wilderness. They call themselves Corps of Discovery. Their boats are docked at St. Charles this very minute. I talked to a few men today who actually tried to sign on with the expedition. Of course, they'll choose only a few and those will be top-grade men." He shook his head in thought. "I didn't get to the hotel today but some say they make quite a pair. They are both tall and as strong as ten-year oaks. They said when Clark took off his hat that red hair of his was so bright it looked as if his head was on fire." He shook his head and laughed.

I said nothing, continuing reading my book.

Uncle Abner glanced over to me and frowned. "Davey, are you all right? You haven't said two words all night." He laid his paper aside and walked over to me.

"Nothing's wrong, Uncle Abner," I answered. "I'm just not quite as excited about it as I was."

"And why is that? That's all you've talked about for weeks now."

I looked up. His shadow loomed tall on the wall from the oil lamp. "I guess I might as well tell you. I tried to sign on with the expedition today at the Parker Hotel."

"You did what?" Uncle Abner asked.

"I played hooky and waited for hours to get a look at Lewis and Clark. I've never seen two men like them," I said excitedly. "You could tell just by looking at them that there is greatness in them."

Uncle Abner lit his pipe and pulled up a chair to listen to me. "Go on, Davey. I want to hear everything about those two explorers."

"Well, everyone interested in signing up for the expedition was supposed to line up and talk to a Sergeant Riley

who they left in charge. I waited in line a long time and..."
I paused and looked away.

"They wouldn't take you would they, Davey?" Uncle Abner asked.

I shook my head. "No. When he found out my age he wanted nothing to do with me."

"You really didn't think you'd have a chance to sign on, did you, Davey, boy?"

I shrugged. "I thought there might be a chance. I could handle myself just as good as any man going...maybe better." My chin jutted forward in determination.

"But, what about school? You've got years ahead of you to try something like that," Uncle Abner argued.

I shook my head. "I want to go with them. I want to explore that part of the United States." I lowered my eyes. "I don't belong in the city, Uncle Abner. I feel like a fish out of water. The kids at school don't like me. Even Master Boggs seems to have something against me. There's nothing about St. Louis I like." I bit into my lower lip. "I want to get back to the wilderness."

Uncle Abner shook his head sadly. "It looks as if your Aunt Maude and I have failed you, Davey. And when we fail you, we've failed your Ma and Pa, God rest their souls."

Looking up, I saw the hurt in his eyes. I got up from my stool and placed my arm around his shoulder. "That's not true, Uncle Abner. It's not you; it's the city. I'm not made to be a storekeeper. I'll never be happy until I'm back where I belong."

"And you think you belong on this expedition into this unexplored land?" Uncle Abner asked.

"Yes, I do."

"Didn't they tell you of the hardships and danger you'd have?" he asked, letting a stream of gray smoke seep from his lips.

"They told me all that. I still want to go. I know I could do it. I know I have to have a chance."

Uncle Abner sighed. "Well, I guess we could talk about it until the cows came home and the answer would still be the same. You want to go but you can't because you're too young. Is that right?"

I nodded.

"Until the time comes when you are eighteen or old enough to be out on your own, your Aunt Maude and I will try to make you happy here." He tapped his pipe on the bottom of his shoe. "That's about all we can do for now."

I nodded sadly and returned to my book. Uncle Abner got up, stretched, and went back to his chair by the lantern to finish his paper. Suddenly, I thought of something. "Uncle Abner, if I was to some way get them to take me, would you let me go? I mean, if you had to sign a document of permission, would you do it?"

Uncle Abner bit down on his pipe and thought for a few moments. Finally, he smiled and nodded his head. "Yes, lad. If you get Lewis and Clark to say you can go, I won't be the one to stand in your way. I'll even talk myself blue and convince your Aunt Maude."

I screamed and ran over to hug the huge man. "Thank you, Uncle Abner," I cried. "Thank you a lot!"

Chapter 4

Rubbing my arms, I shivered. The May nights were still cold. I sniffled and ran my hand along Snooker's back. My eyes had not left the window on the northeast corner of the second floor of the Parker Hotel. That was the room of Lewis and Clark. I tried time and again to gain entrance by the stairs inside only to be thrown out again and again.

Tonight, I had another plan to talk to the two explorers. Nervously, I tapped a finger along a wooden rung of the ladder propped next to the window. I knew they were making frantic plans to depart for St. Charles in two days. It would be my last chance.

Blowing on my hands, I flexed my stiff fingers. "I'm freezing to death out here, Snooker," I whispered. "It must be close to midnight." Looking up, I saw a yellow circle surrounding a full moon. "If Uncle Abner and Aunt Maude knew what I was up to they'd skin me alive." I couldn't help the sly smile that came to my lips in the darkness.

I jumped to my feet as a dim light flowed through the film of curtain covering the window. My heart pounded in my chest and my mouth was so dry I couldn't swallow. A silhouette streaked by the curtain. I couldn't tell if it was Captain Lewis or Lieutenant Clark.

Placing my foot on the bottom rung, the old ladder creaked beneath my weight. Slowly, carefully, I inched my way up. My breathing pumped with excitement. Counting the steps to number fourteen, I knew I was at the top and even with the window. Pausing, I craned my neck to see inside. Leaning to one side, I tried getting a better look.

The ladder started to slide like butter along the wall. Grunting, I tried to pull it back into place, but it was too late. It streaked along the wall and off the corner of the building crashing into a row of bushes at the bottom. I lunged back grabbing the window ledge and was left dangling in mid-air.

At the bottom, Snooker ran back and forth looking up at me. I bit into my lip as he barked loud enough to wake the dead. Kicking the open air, my fingers started to slip from the narrow ledge. I swallowed my pride. "Help!" I called. "Help! Someone, help me!"

Snooker ran frantically below barking.

I struggled to get a toe hold on the smooth wall of the hotel building. "Help! Help!" I called once more.

The window slid open and a head poked through it.

"What in the name of...?"

I recognized Lieutenant Clark's voice.

"Would you look what we have here, Merriweather? We've caught ourselves a peeping Thomas," he said.

Looking up, I smiled. I was thankful it was dark.

"Please, Lieutenant Clark, I just want to speak to you and Captain Lewis."

Snooker continued barking furiously from below.

"I should let you drop, young fellow. You may have had plans to rob us or worse," Clark said.

"I swear," I said. "I just want to talk to you." I heard muffled voices as Clark turned to talk to Lewis.

I prayed they'd make a decision soon knowing in just seconds my grasp would give way and I'd fall two stories into the bushes below.

"We'll save your neck for the sheriff, young fellow. You've got some explaining to do," Lewis said.

They pulled me through the window and slammed me roughly to the floor. I looked up with a weak smile on my face into the accusing eyes of Lewis and Clark.

I tipped my hat. "Davey Hutchins at your service, sirs."

"At your service, indeed," scolded Lewis. "I've a mind to throw you head first out of the window."

Holding up my hand, I quickly tried to sort my thoughts. Things weren't going as I planned. "Please, I beg you. Give me a chance to explain."

"I don't think there's anything much to explain. The facts are right here for everyone to see. You are trying to rob us," Lewis said.

I shook my head. "No, sir. I would never do anything like that to either of you. In fact, I wouldn't do anything like that to anyone."

Clark turned to Lewis. "I've got to admit," he said, "the boy doesn't look like a thief."

"Sirs, if I planned to rob you, why would I bring my dog? I mean, it wouldn't be very smart to bring a dog who barks like that."

Lewis furrowed his thick brows for a few moments in thought. "That's true. But, who's to say that that dog down there is yours? It could be just a dog who happened by."

I buried my face in my hands shaking my head. "No. You don't understand. I tried to come up to your room by the stairs but the hotel man threw me out five times."

"And if we were to believe this...What is it that a boy like you would have to talk to us about?" Clark asked.

I swallowed deep and stood on my feet. I wiped my sweaty hands along my breeches. "Sirs, Captain Lewis and Lieutenant Clark, I want more than anything in the entire world to go with you on the expedition." I hurried on with my explanation. "I could do a lot of things for you. I promise."

"Didn't Sergeant Riley tell you that we couldn't endanger a boy on a trip like this?" Clark asked.

I nodded. "Yes, sir. I tried to sign up yesterday but he told me it was impossible."

"Well, then, you know that it's impossible," Lewis said.

"Do you mean you're not allowed to take a boy along?" I asked.

Clark shrugged. "I don't think there's any specific age

minimum. We do have a youth signed on who's eighteen. But that's legal age of manhood. Men go to war at that age."

"Sirs, I'm a crack shot. I can hunt and trap with the best of them. I've worked outdoors all my life. I've hardly ever been to town except for the last three months I've lived in St. Louis with my Aunt and Uncle."

"And where are your parents, boy?" Clark asked, running his fingers through his bush of red hair.

"Both dead," I said solemnly. "Pa and I had a ten acre farm. I came here to live with Uncle Abner and Aunt Maude after he died."

"Then you've got a good home. You can be thankful for that, at least," Lewis said.

"I suppose so," I said sadly. "I don't like the city. I don't like school. I want to go out into the wilderness again. My Uncle Abner wants me to learn to be a shopkeeper." I shook my head. "I'll always be a farmer."

Clark glanced over to Lewis with a look of understanding in his pale blue eyes. He turned back. "And what all could you do if, by some miracle, we should decide to take you?"

My heart started to pound. I smiled. "Sirs, I could help pole the boat. I could help put up and break camp. I could shoot game, fish, trap...anything that would help you. Anything you'd want me to."

"What parent or guardian for that matter would allow a boy your age to go on such a dangerous mission?" Lewis asked.

"Uncle Abner said that if I could get your permission to sign on with the expedition he would sign the proper documents giving his permission for me to go."

Clark scratched his head. "We've already signed on the allotted twenty-eight men. By rights we don't have room for any more."

My heart sank into my boots. "Oh..."

"Stand up straight, boy. Throw those shoulders back and let's have a look at you," Clark ordered.

I did as I was told. Throwing my shoulders back, I sucked in my stomach and looked straight ahead. Clark felt the cords of muscle in my upper arms and noticed the breadth of my shoulders.

"You're not puny, that's for sure," he said quietly.

Lewis nodded for Clark to come to the other part of the room. They talked quietly to one another. I stood there with my hat in my hand.

Lewis snapped his suspenders a time or two in deliberation. Clark shook his head, shrugged, nodded and coughed. At last they looked back over to me and turned.

"You know, of course," Lewis said, "that this isn't a kids' campout. You'll be gone for months. No one knows what sort of dangers lie out there. You'll be cold, sick, and wet much of the time. There won't be any feather beds to sleep on or piping hot pies baked by Aunt Maude. We won't have time to heat water for bathing. Your clothes will likely be threadbare by the time you get back...if you get back. They'll be snow and ice and rain. Mosquitoes will drain you of your blood. Wild animals are liable to prey on you. Tribes of Indians or groups of people yet unknown may pounce on you in the night. No one may come back alive. If you get out of hand it will be a swift kick in the rear-end for you. When you are issued an order you will obey immediately without question. Your duties will tend to be trivial and mundane. No fancy logging, mapping, and ordering people about for you. You'll have to wash our clothes, fix our food, pitch our tents, wash our utensils...things like that. An Indian may have your scalp on his wikkiup by this time next month."

He leaned closer to me looking me straight in the eyes. "Now, do you still want to go?" he asked.

Clark pitched forward on the soles of his feet waiting for my answer.

"Yes, sir. I sure do," I answered without one moment's delay.

Lewis looked back at Clark and they broke into uproarious laughter.

I nodded and smiled. "Yes, sir. I sure do," I repeated.

Clark, wiping the tears of laughter from his eyes, clapped me on the shoulder. "All right, lad. We've had a man get sick on us and cancel out. He was supposed to be the kind who would do a lot of the chores we talked to you about." He looked at me. "So, we'll give you papers tonight and if you can get your Uncle to sign them, we'll take you."

I stood there for several moments, speechless. Finally, I gasped. "You mean I can go? If Uncle Abner signs the permission forms, you'll let me go along?"

Lewis and Clark smiled and nodded.

"Yaaahooo!" I shouted throwing my hat into the air hitting the ceiling. I rushed to the two men and embraced them one at a time forgetting their importance for the moment. At last, I remembered and backed shyly away. "I...I'm sorry. I didn't..."

"Never mind, Davey," Clark said smiling. "You've got a perfect right to be excited. This is a chance any boy would give his life for."

"Now, take these papers and get out of here so we can get some sleep. If everything is in order, you can meet us in St. Charles on May twenty-first. Is that clear?" Lewis asked in a serious tone.

"Yes, sir. I understand completely." I took the papers from Lewis and started toward the window.

"Say, lad. This time you can use the stairs. That might be a real big step," Lewis said, laughing.

"Oh, yeah." I grinned sheepishly and turned toward the door. I paused for a moment. "I hate to ask you sirs, after you've been so kind and all. Would there be any chance for me to take my dog, Snooker? He's great out in the wide open."

Lewis and Clark shrugged. "I don't see why not. After

all, a man has got to have his dog with him. Right, Davey?" Clark asked chuckling.

He jostled my shoulder. "That's right, sir. That's totally right," I said throwing my hat into the air once again.

"Now, be off with you so we can get to bed and get some sleep," Lewis said, trying to sound stern.

"Yes, sir. I'm going. Sleep well, sirs, sleep well." I closed the door quietly after me and then shouted loud enough to wake every occupant in the hotel. People ran to their doors in their nightshirts and watched me shouting and racing down the steps two at a time!

Chapter 5

I still couldn't believe my good fortune. I lay there in bed staring at the ceiling thinking of what might lie ahead. I saw myself finding treasures and becoming instantly rich. I even saw myself saving the lives of the famous explorers.

Uncle Abner couldn't believe his eyes when I showed him the documents that morning with the illustrious presidential seal and the signatures of Lewis and Clark. For a moment he was angry when he learned I had disobeyed him and was at the hotel dangerously dangling from a second story window ledge when I should have been in bed. But, the feeling was fleeting when he looked into my excited face.

Uncle Abner signed the documents of permission all the while wiping his eyes and blowing his nose. He honored his promise and muttered something about 'He hoped his beloved dead brother would understand and approve.'

Aunt Maude was not as gracious. At first she absolutely refused to listen to anything so absurd. "A boy should get an education. A boy needed guiding and watching. A boy needed stern discipline. A boy needed tending. Who would see that he ate right? Who would take care of him when he got sick? Who would mend his torn clothing? Who would see that he read his Bible regularly?"

After a long time of crying, persuading, and warning, she fled to her room to nurse a "torturous" headache upon her feather bed. Uncle Abner smiled and gave me a masculine wink.

###

"Hutchins!"

I jumped and yelped as once again Master Boggs cracked me across the knuckles with his hickory stick.

"Are you daydreaming again, Hutchins?" The schoolmaster asked, placing his hands on his hips. "It isn't enough that you play hooky every other day and refuse to study."

Smiling, I focused my attention on the loose flap of skin wiggling on his throat. I thought it looked like a turkey's wattle.

"I'm sorry, Master Boggs," I said. "I guess I was thinking about something else."

"That fact is obvious. A 'bumpkin' like you should value an education more than any of us. You are very lucky to be able to go to school."

"Yes, sir. I do feel lucky today."

The schoolmaster's brows arched. "Perhaps, you would remove that smirk from your face if I told you that I wanted you to stay after school and copy the entire Declaration of Independence one hundred times. Would that remove the smile from your face, Hutchins?"

I thought for a moment and then grinned from one ear to the other. "I don't think it would, Master Boggs."

The schoolmaster huffed and snorted. His face turned crimson and his beady gray eyes seemed to smoke behind the little square spectacles. He raised the hickory stick and whacked me across the hands once again.

I looked up and grinned.

"Are you defying me, young man? Are you doing this to make me angry? Because if you are, you are succeeding." He raised the stick and aimed for my knuckles once again.

This time I caught the stick in mid-air and jerked it out of his hand. I got to my feet and broke the weapon across my knee handing the two pieces back to him.

Master Boggs was enraged. His face turned a bright

red and then purple. "I'll...I'll have you expelled for this, you young hoodlum!"

"You'd do that to one of the members of the famous Lewis and Clark expedition?"

Master Boggs swung around, his mouth wide open. He couldn't believe that anyone would have the gall to call out without raising her hand.

"Prissy," he said, "I'm surprised at you. You've never spoken out like that before. This young scoundrel is having a terrible influence on the entire class."

Prissy got up from her seat. Her hands were clenched into fists. Her cheeks were flushed a deep pink.

"Didn't you hear what I said, Master Boggs?" she asked.

"Of course I heard what you said, Prissy. You said: 'You'd do that to one of the members of the famous Lewis and Clark expedition?' The skinny schoolmaster's mouth dropped open showing the front gold tooth. Turning around, he looked down at me.

Master Boggs turned back to Prissy. "Explain yourself young lady. What do you mean by those words?"

"I mean just what I said. My father told me that it was racing across St. Louis like wildfire." She looked over at me and smiled. "That boy whom you've made fun of and hit with that terrible stick time and time again is a member of the Lewis and Clark expedition. He leaves day after tomorrow to travel to St. Charles to begin exploring the new lands."

Master Boggs' face turned pale as the blood drained from it. "Is what she is saying true, Mister Hutchins? Are you really going on the expedition with Lewis and Clark? Surely there must be some mistake."

I sat there not saying a word. Every student scooted forward to the edge of his seat.

I smiled and looked up into the schoolmaster's beady eyes. My voice was clear as a bell. "No, sir, there's no mistake."

Shouts and cries broke out in the schoolroom. Students rushed from their seats to pound me on the back. Some brought pieces of paper for me to sign. Today, I was the most honored student in the classroom.

Master Boggs shouted for order. At last he threw the two pieces of the hickory stick into the air and pounded me on the back himself.

I felt I could float right off my bench. I noticed, as I looked over the shoulders and through the tangle of arms and legs, that one person was sitting silently in her seat. Prissy James was anything but happy.

I sat on the grass next to Prissy watching her fingers trace through Snooker's hair.

Prissy looked up and smiled. Her lower lip quivered and her lashes fluttered. "Well, I guess you got your wish, Davey. You said if you ever got the chance to leave St. Louis, you'd take it in a minute."

I looked at her. "Yes, I guess I did. I'm happy about it except for one thing."

Prissy looked me in the eyes. "Oh, and what is that?"

I was unable to meet her direct gaze. "I want to go in the worst way possible. I can hardly wait to get started except..."

"Except for what, Davey?"

"Except I hate like everything that I won't see you for a long time."

Prissy's face turned red but I knew she was pleased.

"I feel the same way, Davey," she said quietly.

"I'll be back. I promise. I'll be back and we can see each other a whole lot."

"I've heard that this trip is terribly dangerous. No one knows what terrible things are out there. There are savages, wild animals, diseases..." She shuddered. "It scares me to think of them."

34

"Yes," I admitted, "there could be a lot of those things. But, there may also be riches, new waterways to the Pacific Ocean, new civilizations to discover..."

She shook her head. "I don't care about those things. I want you to come back safely. I don't want you hurt or...even worse."

I shrugged. "Ah, I'm pretty tough. I can take care of myself."

She looked up, her eyes clouded with tears. "When do you leave from St. Charles?"

"Captain Lewis said to be at the harbor at 4:00 a.m. sharp with all of my gear."

Prissy fondled Snooker's ears. "I know Snooker will miss you."

I shook my head. "No. Snooker is going along. He'll be the only animal except for horses on the expedition."

"Oh, that's wonderful...for Snooker, that is."

I sighed and looked at the sun slowly setting behind a bank of hills. "I suppose I'd better go. I've got some packing to do. Aunt Maude wanted me home early tonight. She's planning a big family supper."

Prissy got to her feet brushing the grass from her dress. She looked up and smiled. "Of course, I shouldn't be keeping you."

Looking down, I poked the ground with the toe of my boot.

"Davey, you won't forget me when you're out there, will you?"

I smiled, shaking my head. "How could I forget anyone as nice as you?"

Prissy reached beneath her hair. "I want to be sure you won't forget me."

She handed me a gold chain. "You want me to have this?" I asked.

"I'd be happy if you'd accept it. My picture is inside the locket."

I unsnapped the locket and looked at the miniature handpainted portrait of her. My heart thumped in my chest. "It's beautiful. I'll carry it with me everywhere I go."

"I would like that," she said.

Reaching out, I took her hand. "This locket and your picture will see me through everything. Someday, I'll bring it back to you."

"Oh, I hope so." Prissy blushed and squeezed my hand. "You go and get this adventure out of your system, Davey. I'll be here when you come back. I'll be waiting for you to tell me about the most wonderful adventure known to man. And I'll be proud that Davey Hutchins was a member of that expedition!"

Chapter 6

Uncle Abner pulled the bulging valise from the pony cart and set it on the ground. The fog settled in thick and damp. The river was barely visible from where we stood. I wore heavy clothing and fur-lined boots and gloves. I tied a scarf over my ears and pulled a beaver-skin hat down over my head.

The sounds of the river's current and of hectic activity seeped from the thick fog. I recognized the graveled voice of Sergeant Riley.

"Well, I guess this is it, Davey, boy," Uncle Abner said. "It looks as though you're really going through with it. I heard you pacing the floor all night long afraid you'd over-sleep."

I nodded, lifting Snooker from the cart. "I'm going through with it, sir. We're supposed to pull out at five o'clock."

Uncle Abner looked toward the river. "You can still back out of this, boy. We could hop right in the cart and be home this time tomorrow sitting down to your Aunt Maude's cornbread biscuits, country ham, and fried eggs."

I grinned. "That sounds good. But, it would take more than a great breakfast to make me back out of this."

Uncle Abner nodded regretfully and smiled. "I know it would, lad. You've got a lot of your father in you and you should be proud of it."

Uncle Abner pointed to the valise. "I guess your Aunt Maude packed you plenty of warm clothing. She was up most of Friday night fretting that she would forget something."

"She's wonderful, Uncle Abner. You tell her for me that I love her and always will."

"I will, boy. She'll cry until the middle of next Tuesday when she hears it. But, she'll be as warm and happy as an oven inside."

Glancing toward the river, I shifted my feet nervously.

"I know you're eager to get aboard and I won't keep you but another minute." He swiped at his drooling nose. "I just want you to take care of yourself. I want you to come back here someday when it's all over." He shook his head. "Not to live here or make your living or anything. Just come visit your Aunt Maude and me. You're like the son we never had."

I put out my hand and Uncle Abner shook it warmly. Without a word, he pulled me to him and pressed me so tight I had a hard time breathing. I inhaled the comforting smell of his tobacco. I wanted to stay there a long time, all safe, but I knew it was time to go.

Pushing myself away, I bit into my lower lip to curb my wavering emotions. "I guess I'd better be getting down there. I don't want to be late my first day on duty."

"Right you are, lad. I'll be on my way so you can tend to things." Uncle Abner turned and stepped up into the cart. He looked down at me through the darkness. "We're all proud of you, Davey," He flicked the reins. The cart jolted forward, grinding small pebbles beneath its wheels.

With a grunt, I lifted my valise from the ground and started to walk down the rough incline to the river.

As my eyes adjusted to the fog and darkness, I saw the outline of the big vessel waiting at the river's edge. Men rushed back and forth across planks to load her. They cursed and yelled and a few started to sing an old sea chant. At once I was caught up in the excitement, adventure, and thrill of the moment and the promise of what was to come.

"Put your gear down over there, fella, and start to load those boxes. You signed on to work, not take a leisure cruise down the river."

Turning, I looked up into the bearded face of Sergeant Riley. "Yes, sir," I squeaked.

Through the fog I saw a sly grin beneath the Sergeant's beard. "Well, I do believe I recognize that weak little voice. It seems to me it comes from a boy who pestered me until I blew my stack the other day. Is that you, Davey Hutchins?"

My mouth became dry and I forced my voice to deepen. "Yes, sir, Sergeant Riley. I'm Davey Hutchins. I'm the same Davey Hutchins who tried to sign on at the Parker Hotel last week."

"So you are. I heard that you wheedled and whined your way to go." He shook his head. "A real story you must have told Captain Lewis and Captain Clark."

This was the first time I had heard of Clark being referred to as Captain. I learned later that since he was to be co-leader they thought the rank should be equal.

"Everything I told the Captains was the truth, Sergeant," I replied.

Sergeant Riley reached out and grabbed me by the collar. He lifted me to my tiptoes. "I don't believe you, boy. You made up stories as big as mountains and preyed on the good Captains' sympathies. And worse than that, you went over my head. You talked to the Captains on your own. That made me look bad in their eyes."

He shook me hard.

"That makes me real mad. I don't like someone to go over my head, especially not a wet-nosed kid."

Snooker started to bark when he saw me being man-handled. He yipped and yiped around the Sergeant's legs. Sergeant Riley kicked at him. Snooker caught a boot in the side and yelped tumbling back.

"Get that blasted dog away or he'll be dead before you can say 'Jack Robinson'."

"Snooker! Get back!" I ordered.

Snooker came back barking and growling at the Sergeant's legs.

"You might as well know right off that it's going to be a hard trip for you, Hutchins. I'm going to drive you until you drop. You'll be doing all of the dirtiest jobs I can find and if you complain I'll tend to you personally." He shook me again. "Is that understood?"

I hit out with my fists. Snooker came up from behind and sank his sharp teeth into the meat of the Sergeant's calf.

"Yipe! Balls of fire!"

Sergeant Riley released me and started to chase Snooker around and around in a circle.

"What is going on here, Sergeant Riley?"

Sergeant Riley came to an attention.

"It's not time to play with a dog," Captain Lewis reprimanded. "This is serious business. Do you understand?" he asked.

"Yes, sir. I understand, sir," he said, trying to control his anger.

Lewis looked down. "And is that you, Davey Hutchins?"

I grinned. "Yes, sir. I'm ready to board, sir."

"You'll board when I say to board," he said sharply. "Right now I want you to put your valise on the boat and give these men a hand loading the supplies. Is that understood?"

"Yes, sir. I understand," I said.

"Good." His voice softened. "I thought you would. I wouldn't have agreed on you coming if I had had one reservation about you." He looked over to Sergeant Riley rubbing his leg. "And now Sergeant, you take care of this boy and see that he gets his gear on board. Then assign him to some duty helping load."

"Yes, sir," said Sergeant Riley.

Captain Lewis wheeled around and started back to the boat. He halted in his tracks and looked back over his shoulder. "Oh, yes...and Sergeant see that his dog is properly taken care of and fed. He'll be making the trip with us."

"Yes, sir," Sergeant Riley said grinding his teeth together.

Chapter 7

The fog was as thick as pea soup when the keelboat and the two flatbottom boats called pirogues set sail down the Missouri. I sat huddled on a box filled with quilts and watched the harbor disappear from view. Everyone was eerily silent as the boat pulled out. Each one knew that he may never return.

Sergeant Riley pulled nervously at his chin whiskers.

Captain Lewis braced himself against the morning chill. He looked straight ahead with anticipation. It had taken months of preparation. Now the great test began.

Captain Clark pulled his beaver skin cap down over his ears. He looked like a stone statue he was so still.

All of the men were caught up in their private thoughts and prayers.

A hard lump formed at the base of my throat. My fingers fumbled into my coat pocket and pulled out the locket.

###

I got a good look at the vessel when the day's sun had burned away the fog. The keelboat was quite a boat, I thought. Captain Lewis had it made to his own specifications. It had an iron frame and was covered with birch bark. It was fifty-five feet long, four and one-half feet in beam, and twenty-six inches deep. Lewis calculated that it was capable of carrying eight thousand pounds. It had ten-foot decks fore and aft, with a fore-castle and an after cabin. Amidships, the gunwales were backed by stout wooden lockers that could be raised to make them higher in the event of an Indian attack from either shore. There was also a huge tarpaulin that could be fastened into place in a matter of minutes that would protect us from high waters. The vessel itself could be poled or rowed. There was also a sail mounted on a thick stumpy mast for the stretches.

I was awestruck by its hugeness and complexity. Most of the first morning was spent exploring it from stem to stern.

At mid-morning Lewis ordered a whiskey cask opened to "take the chill off our bones" as he said. One dipper per hand was rationed. The men eagerly grouped around the barrel rubbing their hands together and licking their lips. Many of the hands were rough and ready fellows and had been through many warring campaigns.

I sat hunched on a box as the cold wind whipped my face. The men drank and laughed as they passed the dipper from one to the other.

"Put the bung back into the cask, Tandy," ordered Captain Lewis. "Everyone has had a drink and has got his blood circulating again."

"Just a minute, Captain Lewis, sir," Sergeant Riley said with a sly smile. "There's one hand who hasn't had a taste of the rye yet."

Heads turned to look at me.

"He's a might young for it, Sergeant," Captain Lewis said, looking over at me.

"Why not ask him, Captain? He can always say, no. I mean, he may want to warm his innards a little just like the rest of us."

A mumble ran through the men supporting Riley's suggestion.

"Very well, Sergeant, ask young Hutchins. But remember, it's up to him. I'll not allow any coercion," he said harshly.

"Right you are, Captain. It'll be entirely up to the boy," Riley assured him.

Captain Lewis nodded and walked into his cabin to confer with Clark about a map.

Once the cabin door was closed, Sergeant Riley

44

grinned showing his stained teeth. "Hey, lad," he called.

Looking up, I obeyed at once. "Yes, sir, Sergeant."

Everyone grouped around ready for the fun.

"We have been real impolite, Hutchins. The Captain has been so kind as to allow us one dipper of rye whiskey from the barrel to celebrate our departure as well as break the chill, and we forgot you."

I looked up at the circle of men surrounding me. I saw good natured grins and sly smiles on their faces.

"We've all had our drink and now it's your turn, lad," Sergeant Riley said, poking a man next to him with his elbow.

"I...I don't think so, Sergeant. I'm not that chilled. I've got a good fur-lined coat on and gloves."

Sergeant Riley nodded. "That's true and so do we. But, it's the chill that gets inside that a body needs to take care of."

I shook my head.

"Well, now, are you telling us that you're man enough to sign on this long and dangerous venture. But, you're not man enough to swallow a dipper of whiskey?"

He looked around and grinned at the rest of the men. "Maybe you just don't like our company." The Sergeant pretended to be hurt. "Is that it?"

"It's not that," I said quietly.

"What, then? Maybe you've never had a taste of it before in your young life. Could that be it, lad?"

I looked at the men seeing the look of dare in their eyes. "I...I had it a few times." I flinched knowing I would have been skinned alive by my Pa or Aunt Maude if ever I had more than a spoonful for medicinal purposes.

"Well, then, it's settled." Sergeant Riley pulled the bung from the cask and filled the dipper brim full. He handed the dipper to me. "There you go, lad. It goes down the best in a few hard gulps rather than little sips like a lady at a tea party."

I took the dipper and smelled it and my eyes watered. The men watched me closely. I knew that this was my first test. Sergeant Riley hadn't wasted any time.

"Up it goes, lad. Swallow it all," Riley ordered.

"Go ahead, Davey," someone said, poking my shoulder.

"Show him, Davey," another said.

Bringing the dipper to my mouth, I closed my eyes and held my breath. Quickly, I tipped it up and allowed the whiskey to flow down my throat. In the back of my mind I heard the men cheer and slap me on the back. But the only thing I was aware of was the blazing hot liquid flowing down my throat causing my insides to burn like fire.

My breath caught and I gasped, but I up-ended the dipper and drained it of the last drop. At last I looked up, smiled, belched, and handed the empty dipper back to Sergeant Riley.

"Thank you, Sergeant," I gasped. "That...that really did warm my insides."

The sly grin dropped from Riley's face and his brows furrowed in disappointment.

The men cheered and pounded me on the back.

"All of you back to work!" Riley ordered sharply. "There's plenty of work left to do. Get going or I'll throw you all head first into the river!"

Men scattered in all directions and went back to work. My head spun and the flames smouldered in my stomach. Carefully, I moved behind a pile of boxes out of view and lowered myself to the deck. In a matter of minutes I was sleeping soundly with Snooker curled at my side.

It was late afternoon when I awoke to the shouts and cries from the crew.

Opening my eyes, I groaned. Unsteadily, I got up and walked out from behind the boxes.

46

The keelboat was anchored and tied to the shore and men were fishing off the bow of it as well as the flat bottom boats. I saw bent backs and strained faces as they pulled in huge catfish.

No sooner had their lines hit the water than the bait was taken and the fish were hooked.

Walking over, I looked at the mound of huge fish. Some were wiggling and some were already stiff. Many of them weighed close to a hundred pounds. The men, Lewis and Clark included, were having a wonderful time pulling in these huge beasts.

Snooker ran excitedly about sniffing the fish. Now and then one flopped in his face and he yelped and backed away.

I forgot my head and stomach in the excitement and hurried over to watch a group of men.

One man looked up and grinned. I liked him instantly. His grizzled, weatherbeaten face was etched with a million wrinkles. A corncob pipe stuck out of the corner of his mouth and a mist of gray smoke curled from it. He motioned for me to take the pole.

"Here you go, lad," he said. "Try your luck. I've already caught enough to feed us for a week or more."

"Thank you," I said.

"We're using smaller fish for bait. Even the bait runs up close to a pound a piece." He shook his head. "I never saw the likes of these catfish."

Raising the pole, I threw my line into the water.

The old man nodded his approval. "That's a good spot, lad. Just wait a bit and you're sure to hook one."

I nodded, keeping an eye on the line.

"How's the first day going for you, lad?" he asked.

"It's going fine, sir," I replied.

The man grinned and shook his head. "Don't call me sir. I'm just the Cookie around here. I'm no officer or gentleman." He pulled the pipe from his teeth and the smoke sifted from his parted lips. "I signed on to feed this crew." He smiled. "The Sergeant said you're to give me a hand at times."

"Yes, I am. I'm supposed to do a bit of everything, I guess."

The man put out his hand. "My name's Theodore P. Pomroy. My friends call me Teddy."

I shook his hand. "My name's Davey Hutchins. Pleased to meet you, Teddy."

"The same goes for me, Davey," the man said, his eyes crinkling almost to the point of closing.

"I've never cooked much, but I'll do all I can," I said.

"I'm sure you will. There will be no fancy victuals on this trip. We'll hear a lot of mumbling and grumbling but we'll do the best we can and that's that."

I liked the sound of his quiet authority. It had none of the taunting and teasing of Sergeant Riley's.

"You leave a family behind back in St. Louis, boy?" Teddy asked, after a few minutes watching me fish.

"Yes." I shrugged. "Well, not exactly. My Ma and Pa are buried about one hundred miles from St. Louis. I've been living with my Uncle Abner and Aunt Maude there for the past three months."

"The city just started to choke you, huh? Is that right?"

"Yes, that's right. Snooker and I never did seem to fit in the city or the school."

"Everyone's heard of how you wrangled a place on this trip." He laughed. "Climbing a ladder up to the Captains' hotel room. We all admire your spunk, lad."

I grinned. "Thank you. But, I don't think Sergeant Riley admires it."

"Ah, the Sergeant doesn't know a good man when he sees one." He waved his hand.

"Do you think...?" My line went taut. For a few moments the line moved from side to side as the fish toyed with the bait. The water churned. I stood, leaning over the side of the boat, giving the fish as much line as possible. The fish dove to the bottom of the river. I felt the tremendous tug and strength of the huge beast. Another tug hit the line and catapulted me forward losing my balance. I fell head first into the river.

"Davey!" Teddy called. "Can you swim, lad?"

I swallowed a mouthful of muddy water and choked. "Yes, I can swim!" I yelled back. "Don't worry!" My feet slipped on the slick bottom and fell in suspension. The power of the fish pulled me through the water. I couldn't believe the strength of the creature.

Looking back over my shoulder, I saw the men line the side of the boat shouting, waving their fists and calling encouragement. Snooker ran back and forth barking excitedly. Sergeant Riley doubled up with laughter.

Gasping, I went under again swallowing more water. My eyes were open but I saw only inches away because of the murky water. I surfaced, took a gulp of air, submerged, and glided beneath the water still clutching the pole.

This is the biggest fish yet, I told myself. This beauty must weigh over a hundred pounds.

"Hold on, there, Davey! Don't give up! That might be the granddaddy of them all, boy!" Teddy called, shaking his fist.

From the side of the boat, Captains Lewis and Clark watched and yelled right along with the men. I knew I couldn't let this one get away. My reputation depended on it.

"Ride 'em all the way, lad!" Corporal Tandy called.

"I believe you've hooked Jonah, Davey, boy!" Teddy shouted.

I tried to wave but found I needed both hands wrapped around the pole.

The fish was growing tired. It plunged to the bottom of the river. At last, it made a bee-line for the opposite shore and I had no choice but to travel along with it.

The rushing water blotted out all sounds from the boat. "I'll land you, Mr. Catfish," I said. "You can bet I'm not about to let you go. You're going to be cooking over a fire tonight and you're big enough to feed everyone for a week and still have enough left over for Thanksgiving and Christmas dinner." Laughing, I swallowed more water.

I looked up just as the big creature flopped his tail. "Jumping Johosaphat! I've never seen a tail that big!" I shouted.

My feet touched the slick, muddy bottom on the opposite bank. With all my strength I struggled out of the river drenched to the skin. I grabbed hold of the first tree I found lining the bank. Straddling the tree, I propped the pole against it and started to pull the line in. I groaned and grunted feeling the huge weight on the other end. For half an hour I worked the line into the bank.

The huge head surfaced near the bank. Its whiskers were a foot long and its gaping mouth was as wide as a door. I pulled it up onto the bank. The huge creature flopped wildly trying to get back to the river.

"You must weigh over one hundred and twenty-five pounds. You're bigger than anything that's been caught on the boat!"

I looked across the river and with a huge grunt hoisted the fish off the ground. A loud cheer went up on the boat. The men had watched the battle until the end making bets on who would win — me or the mighty catfish.

I had won another victory. I smiled but knew that my luck would have to run out sooner or later. Right now, I had to admit, it felt mighty good!

Chapter 8

The mighty Missouri, which had seemed so gentle and generous at the beginning, became an enemy later on. No one knew what would be around each bend. The river could be slow moving and innocent. Suddenly, it would become swift and treacherous with swirling whirlpools. Tons of mud dropped from banks and rocked the craft. Poling was only possible close to shore. This caused great danger to the crew. Without warning, the bank could collapse and send a huge chunk of mud down upon us.

Some days, through sail, sweeps, or pole we traveled as much as thirty miles. Other days, because of the weather or the river, we were lucky to make five or six miles before we camped.

The expedition never traveled at night. When we camped it was sometimes on river islands. Camping along the bank, we moved back from the edge fearing it would break off during the night. A few of the crew found themselves floating free and had to be rescued.

Driftwood bumped into the keelboat. Sometimes we collided with great timbers looking harmless peeking above the water.

The Missouri was generous and bountiful giving up pike, bass, trout, rockfish, perch, flatback, shrimp, mussels, and the biggest catfish any of us had ever seen.

Captains Lewis and Clark wrote constantly in their diaries. They recorded water depth, color, and speed. They wrote about the nature of the banks, the animals, and plants. The expedition had acquired two horses from a French fur trader. Snooker wasn't the only animal aboard now. Lewis and Clark would follow the craft on horseback along the bank for exercise.

Captain Clark made detailed maps of the entire trip. One day a high wind swept away all his notes and they floated downstream. Another time a bottle of ink spilled when the boat rocked and ruined all his efforts. He never gave up and cheerfully started again. His ruddy face was usually creased in a wide grin.

All hands, who could write, kept diaries as well. I wrote in mine each night. I described the winding river and its uncertain banks. I told about the huge catfish and the river jumping with life. I described the members of the crew especially Lewis, Clark, Teddy, and Tandy the eighteen-year-old corporal.

As the boats passed streams and rivers emptying into the Great Missouri, Lewis and Clark named them so they could be identified on the maps. Sometimes, they let me name them. I called one Sandy River, Smoky River, and Lost River by the way they appeared to me. I described the birds in my diary I saw along the Missouri shore: the long-necked cranes, mud ducks, prairie chickens, pheasants, quail, and herons.

One day the Corps of Discovery came upon a hunting party of Kickapoo Indians. Lewis and Clark bought four deer from them, paying them with two mirrors and a bag of beads. Later on, our own party went out on a hunt bringing back a black bear, two deer, an elk, and reported seeing great herds of buffalo.

The expedition passed various small clusters of Indians. The Mandans had small villages along the Missouri and were happy people. They waved as the boat passed by. The crew kept hearing tales from trappers of the Sioux who were reported to be war-like. We kept a wary eye.

After forty-four days of travel, we arrived at a river they called the Kansas River after the Indians who lived along the banks. At the end of the seventieth day we sailed by the Great Platte River. By this time we had traveled six hundred miles into the wilderness.

Up to this point no one had had an accident or became seriously ill. There had been a few cases of dysentary, headaches, and boils but nothing serious. Home remedies had taken care of them so far. Captain Lewis did have some medical skills.

I had toughened during these seventy days aboard the keelboat. My face and upper body, open to the sun, were burned a deep brown and were as hard as leather. Teddy taught me well during this time. He taught me how to skin and filet a fish, boil a oppossum, fry bear meat, bake bread over an open campfire, and roast prairie chickens.

I was kept busy with many duties. I didn't have time to think of the folks back home. But sometimes at night, just before I fell into a deep exhausted sleep, I thought back to those days. It seemed like a dream to me. The hordes of people, carts, and carriages. The stores, shops, and hotels. The pretty ladies in long dresses and parasols. The gas-lighted streets. Out here we sometimes traveled for weeks and didn't see another human being. And even then it would be a lone trapper or a small group of Indians on a hunting party.

Sergeant Riley watched me like a hawk; he never let me rest. I "heard" his deep voice in my sleep. "Hutchins, help Cookie! Hutchins, unload those crates! Hutchins, wash the Captains' clothes! Hutchins, mend those tent flaps! Hutchins, climb that tree and see what's over yonder! Hutchins, break camp! Hutchins, put up camp!"

Not once did I disobey him. I was determined not to let him get the best of me. Some of the men felt sorry for me and tried to help me with my chores. I refused, telling them that it was part of the bargain.

The rigorous life of the wildnerness was to my liking. I loved watching the shore roll by. It was exciting to stop the keelboat and try to communicate with the various Indian tribes we met.

But, there was one thing that was hard to get used to

on this trip other than Sergeant Riley. Rats! Hordes of rats had infested the boats. They scurried about freely. I found them racing across the supper table and gnawing at my bed blanket. They ran up my arm when I opened a sack of grain and jumped on my shoulder when I opened a cupboard in the Captains' cabin. Snooker caught a few but couldn't keep up with them.

Teddy hit them on the head with a skillet or stomped on them with his heavy boots or trapped them in a corner with a broom. For every one that was dumped into the river, it seemed as though it was replaced by five or ten more. What we needed, Teddy said, was a good mouser. Cats were very scarce and worth their weight in gold in the wilderness because of this problem.

Yawning, I looked sleepily up from my feather pillow. A fat brown rat stood on its hind legs staring into my eyes. Its nose and whiskers wiggled.

Raising up on one elbow, I raised a metal bin and broke a crust off a loaf of bread. Reaching out, I offered it to the little creature. The rat paused for a few moments debating whether it was safe.

"Come on, take the bread or I'll eat it myself," I said.

The rat scurried closer and stood on its hind legs. Its eyes were black as coal. Its nose vibrated as it smelled the bread. "This is your last chance," I warned. I laid the morsel on my palm and the rat crawled onto my hand and nibbled the bread. I didn't like rats at all, but this rat was different, I thought. He had a mark that made him look different from the others. I decided to give him a name.

"I think I'll call you Mr. Jeff after our President, Thomas Jefferson." I nodded my head. "Yes, Mr. Jeff...that's a good name for you," I said breaking another piece of crust from the loaf. "Now, Mr. Jeff, you eat it all up and then you leave me alone. I've got a busy day tomorrow. Teddy wants me up at four to help him start the crew's breakfast."

Mr. Jeff sniffed the air waiting for another piece of bread. When I waved my hand he scurried off the bed.

I watched his tail disappear beneath the door. Smiling to myself, I closed my eyes.

After that, Mr. Jeff became a nightly visitor to my bed. We became good friends. Every night before I fell asleep, Mr. Jeff scampered to my bed, sat on my pillow, and waited for a cracker, piece of bread, or some other morsel. He had a small white spot on his forehead; this made him real special.

Late at night, beneath the light of a candle, I talked to Mr. Jeff about Ma and Pa and sometimes about Prissy. Mr. Jeff trusted me and ran up and down my arm, burrowed beneath my shirt, and perched on my shoulder. He was as much my pet as was Snooker.

One morning I was sleeping soundly dreaming of the farm back in Missouri, when a hard whack of a broom hit my shoulder.

"Yipe!" I yelled sitting straight up in bed.

"Jumpin' jackrabbits! Things are really getting out of hand!"

Blinking my eyes, I looked up at Teddy still waving the broom. "What happened? Why in blazes did you hit me with that broom?"

Teddy sat down beside me. "Davey, boy, you won't believe what I just saw." He continued before I could speak. "I saw the biggest, fattest rat crawling up your arm. It wasn't the least bit afraid."

I chuckled. "Oh, you mean Mr. Jeff."

"Mr. Jeff? I mean a rat. A big rat! It was sitting as big as you please right up there on your shoulder. They're getting completely out of control...those pesky varmits!" Teddy replied with a scowl.

Crawling out of bed, I pulled on my breeches. "You saw Mr. Jeff, Teddy. The little guy and I are good friends."

"A rat? You've got a rat for a pet?" Teddy asked, his brow cocked with doubt.

"That's right." Walking over to the wash basin, I splashed water on my face.

"While the whole boat is being run over with those creatures, you make one a pet." He gestured. "They're everywhere. They're in the grain and flour. They jump out of cupboards and storage bins. They race along the deck floor and gunwales. They burrow beneath our stored blankets and spare clothing." He waved his arms about. "They're everywhere. And you have one for a pet."

"That's right," I said, pulling on my boots.

"You must be crazy, boy."

"Maybe I am, Teddy. But the little fella just sort of adopted me. Snooker lets him climb all over him, too."

"You mean Snooker chases those vermin all over the boat, but lets this little creature run up and down him?"

I nodded. "Yes. Snooker knows Mr. Jeff is special."

"And what's so special about him?" Teddy asked. "A rat is a rat. They're all filthy and destructive. The only good rat is a dead rat."

"That's what I used to think. I never had any love for rats before I met Mr. Jeff. I named him Mr. Jeff after our President, Thomas Jefferson."

"Well, all I can say you'd better keep it quiet. Sergeant Riley would like nothing better than to drown all the rats from here to the Pacific Ocean."

"Don't worry. I'm not going to tell him a thing about Mr. Jeff. He'd be out to get him sure if I did."

Teddy shook his head and pulled his beard. "As far as I'm concerned a rat is a rat. But, because you and I are friends, I won't say a word to anyone else especially not to the Sergeant."

I patted Teddy's shoulder. "Thanks, Teddy. I knew I could count on you."

"Now, get a move on. We've got to get that biscuit dough mixed. It's only a couple hours before dawn."

"I'm ready, let's go," I replied eagerly.

One day we were anchored along the Missouri bank and Sergeant Riley and a squad went on patrol. I was taking advantage of Sergent Riley's absence and was catching up on some sleep. Snooker lay snoring on the floor and Mr. Jeff sat on my shoulder nibbling a cracker.

Suddenly, the door opened and Teddy came rushing in breathlessly. "Davey, lad! Get up! Sergeant Riley's back. If he sees you snoozing, he'll have a fit."

Jumping out of bed, I pulled on my boots. Snooker was immediately on his feet. Mr. Jeff scurried off my shoulder and disappeared out the door.

"I'd better get back to cleaning the deck. He's going to expect that job done and I'm not even half finished."

"Right you are, lad," Teddy said, nodding his head.

Rushing out, I started hauling water from the river and pouring it on the deck. I looked up as Lewis and Clark hurried out of their cabin and walked ashore to meet Sergeant Riley and his squad.

With one eye on my mop and the other on the men on shore, I continued mopping the deck. Lewis and Clark shook Sergeant Riley's hand. I hadn't seen the Captains that pleased in days. Perhaps the patrol had found golden idols or a lost civilization, I thought.

Captain Lewis and Captain Clark led the way back to the boat with Sergeant Riley trailing them, his chest puffed out like a turkey gobbler. He held a bag in his hand.

"You've saved the day, Sergeant Riley, not to mention saving the United States government a large sum of money,"

Captain Lewis said, patting the Sergeant's shoulder.

"I'm just trying to do my duty, sir," Sergeant Riley said. He turned his head and spat.

"I don't think we could have finished the expedition unless something was done pretty soon," Clark said smiling.

"I'm glad you're both pleased, sirs."

Sergeant Riley was too busy congratulating himself to notice if I was working or not. He upended the bag and shook it hard.

Leaning on my mop, I stopped to watch. A huge, gray, furry mound rolled out with a shrill howl. It hunched its shoulders and hissed. Its fangs were long and sharp. Its ears lay back flat to its head. The hair on the back of its neck bristled. Its eyes shone like new gold coins.

Snooker barked and darted to the cabin.

Sergeant Riley had brought back the biggest and meanest looking cat I had ever seen.

"The Chief of the Mandans had it, sir. He got it from a trapper about two years ago. Since then the beast has rid every one of their villages of rats. I had to bargain long and hard to get the Chief to part with it. Finally, I offered three quilts, four mirrors, and three bags of beads for it."

"That was a high price but it'll be worth it," Lewis said with a sharp nod.

"I promise you, Captain, there won't be a rat on this boat in two weeks or my name ain't Rasmus J. Riley," said Sergeant Riley proudly.

Clark and Lewis pounded the sergeant on the back once again and stood back watching the cat go to work. In a matter of moments, it caught and killed four rats with little effort.

I got a sick feeling in the pit of my stomach when I thought about Mr. Jeff. It was only a matter of time before the cat would have him too.

Chapter 9

Puffing my chest out, I proudly rode the spirited roan along the bank. At times I waved to Teddy or Tandy on the keelboat, feeling free astride the beautiful stallion. It was Captain Clark's horse and he had given me permission to ride it. I saw the envy and anger in Sergeant Riley's eyes. He had chores lined up for me but Captain Clark countermanded his orders giving me the afternoon off.

Snooker ran alongside the horse also grateful to get off the boat and stretch his legs. Now and then he darted ahead chasing a squirrel or rabbit.

"You'll never catch a rabbit, Snooker. You're too slow for that. You barely nab a rat now and then," I yelled. My mind went back to the boat and to the huge gray cat Sergeant Riley brought back from the Mandan village. The cat had been aboard less than a week and already I noticed a big difference in the amount of rats running across the deck. I knew Mr. Jeff better stay hidden or he'd be on the big cat's menu.

I had to admit it was good not to have a rat pounce on you when you opened a bag of flour or a cupboard door. But, I couldn't help worrying about Mr. Jeff.

I ran my hand along the smooth neck of the roan. The horse pranced majestically and I felt as though I were the Captain of the expedition instead of a young boy doing the most trivial of jobs.

The boat rounded a bend and disappeared. I looked around. It felt as if I were the only human in the world. As far as I could see the river went on and on, bordered by steep, muddy banks and trees.

Looking down, I noticed Snooker wasn't following me. I whistled. "Snooker, boy! Come on, boy. Get back here!"

Pulling the horse up, I looked around. The cover was thick with bushes and trees. I whistled and called again. "Snooker! Snooker! Where are you?"

Gently I nudged the horse forward and pushed into the thick brush bordering the bank. The air was cut off. The whine of mosquitoes circled my head. Birds fluttered in the tree tops as I pushed through the bushes.

"Snooker! Snooker! Where are you, boy?" I yelled.

Reining the horse in again, I looked around. Everything had gotten strangely quiet. The horse scraped the ground nervously with his front hoof.

It happened so fast I didn't have time to think. A body fell from a tree knocking me from the horse. He was on top of me and my breath was cut off. My eyes nearly popped out of their sockets. Looking down with a sly, sinister grin was the biggest, meanest-looking Indian I had ever seen.

Once my wits had returned, I struggled to free myself. I hit, kicked, bucked, bit, and scratched until I grew weak. The Indian was powerful and only tightened his grip around my chest. I knew my scalp would be taken from me at any moment. I closed my eyes, repeated a hurried prayer, and prepared to die.

The Indian raised up and pulled me to my feet by my coat collar. Grabbing the horse's rein, he pulled me and the horse forward.

After a hundred yards of dodging brush, roots, and bushes we came to a clearing. Over a hundred Indians, men, women, and children, were clustered together. A squaw was holding Snooker. Her hand was clamped tightly around his muzzle so he couldn't bark. The men wore hawks' feathers in their hair and their faces were coated with grease. Most of them carried bows and arrows. A few carried rusty muskets.

I was dragged to an old Indian sitting on a blanket smoking a pipe. He had long gray hair hanging down his back. His face was almost black and his skin looked dry enough to tear. When he opened his mouth, I saw not one tooth.

The old Indian chattered excitedly and motioned with his hands. People hurried one way and another when he

spoke. I knew he had to be the Chief. The Indian who captured me pulled my hands together and tied them with a leather thong. I was then lifted back on the horse and Snooker was handed up to me.

Five Indians started forward with the old chief leading. They walked back to the river with me astride Captain Clark's horse. They all talked at once. I didn't understand one word and prayed that tonight I would look back on this as just an exciting adventure.

When we reached the bank, I saw the keelboat anchored ahead of us next to the opposite shore. The craft's swivel guns aimed toward the party of Indians. Captain Clark had already gotten into a small boat with three men, one of them a skilled half-Indian interpreter named Drouillard, and paddled toward us.

Captain Clark, the interpreter, and the two men had their rifles laying across their laps ready if there was need for them. A serious expression coated their faces.

My captors remained silent watching the boat approach the bank. One Indian pulled an arrow out of a quiver and placed it in his bow. I clenched my jaw to keep my teeth from chattering.

Drouillard knew at once whom to address. He put up a brave front purposely showing the Indians he had no fear and was outraged at them capturing me. The men with Clark tightened their grip on their rifles but all of them had good sense not to make a move to fire.

There was a rapid exchange of talk between the interpreter and the Indian Chief. I tensed when I heard the name "Sioux" mentioned several times.

The Indian Chief gestured wildly.

Finally, Captain Clark motioned he wanted to know what was taking place between the two of them.

"Captain Clark," the interpreter said, turning to his superior, "this is Chief Black Buffalo Bull."

Captain Clark bowed graciously. He was sure this

64

party was only a small portion broken off from the main body.

"And Black Buffalo Bull wants you to know he strongly resents you, Captain Lewis, and your men invading his land. He wants you to know that such acts could set off a war."

Captain Clark nodded. "Tell Black Buffalo Bull that we are sorry he is upset. We do not intend to bother him or his people. We are only on an expedition at the request of the Great American White Father, Thomas Jefferson, the Chief of our country. Tell him that our country is the owner of this land after a legal purchase from France."

Drouillard turned to Black Buffalo Bull and relayed Captain Clark's message. The Indian Chief remained expressionless as he listened. Finally, he opened his toothless mouth and talked rapidly, moving his hands about.

Drouillard turned once again to Clark and told him what the Chief had said. "Black Buffalo Bull says that your entry into the land of his forefathers is trespassing whether the great white father purchased it or not. They have lived on these banks for hundreds of years. He says the only way he will allow you to travel on without a war would be for you to give him a token of your regret." Drouillard paused for a few moments in thought. "In other words, Captain, he wants you to buy your way out of this."

"What do you think?" Captain Clark asked. "Should we put up a stand or try to barter our way out?"

The interpreter licked the thick, black mustache coating his upper lip. "Captain, sir, I know these people. I have been up and down this river trapping and trading for years. There are probably at least a hundred or more men somewhere close by. We might be able to take a stand and drive them back. But doing so we might get many of our men killed. I always gave them a few beaver skins or a few mink when they came by and they seemed satisfied. They just want something to show them that you are truly sorry for invading their land."

"But it's not their land any more, Drouillard. The United States government owns this land now."

"That question is debatable in their eyes. They only know that they have lived along these shores for hundreds of years. They are not going to let a piece of paper convince them that they do not own this land. They still believe that this land is theirs and that you do not belong here."

Captain Clark shook his head.

"Besides, Captain, even if we were to get away they would alert other Sioux tribes further down the Missouri and maybe round up a thousand or more Indians. There's no way we could outfight those odds."

Captain Clark regretfully nodded. He pulled off his coonskin hat and wiped his brow with his forearm.

The Indians gasped at the sight of his blazing red hair. They marveled at its bright color as the sun bounced off of it. One Indian stepped forward, reached up, and touched it with awe and respect.

Captain Clark reared back and promptly put his cap back on his head.

Drouillard turned to the Chief and exchanged more words and then went back to Captain Clark.

"First of all, Captain, they think that you have the greatest hair they have ever seen. They call you Chief Fire Hair. Because of your fine red hair they will let you and your men travel on if you give them tobacco, beads, mirrors, and two bags of grain."

Clark's face flushed with a mixture of anger and embarrassment.

Drouillard grinned broadly. The men accompanying Clark tried to look sober but a grin broke out on their faces.

The grins were catching. The Chief showed a toothless smile. His braves grinned and then broke into laughter.

Finally, Clark laughed and stepped forward shaking the old Chief's hand. The tension had been broken mainly due to the thick bush of red hair on Captain Clark's head.

"All right," Clark said. "Tell the Chief we will give him two twists of tabacco, three mirrors, four bags of beads, and two bags of grain."

The interpreter relayed the Captain's bargain to the Chief.

"The Chief is in agreement except for one thing. He would also like to have that fine coat you are wearing."

Clark fondly looked down at his deer skin jacket. He nodded and shrugged out of it handing it to the happy Chief. Black Buffalo Bull put the jacket on and patted it proudly.

"Tell Chief Black Buffalo Bull we have met his conditions and now we expect no further trouble from his people as we venture on down the Missouri."

Drouillard told the Chief what Clark had said and the Chief smiled and nodded agreeably.

An Indian warrior pulled me from the horse and sliced through the leather strap around my wrists.

"And now, go back and get the items we bartered for the Chief," Captain Clark told two of the men. "We will stay here until the entire transaction is over to show our good fatih."

"And then as I rode into the thick wooded area looking for Snooker, this huge Indian Warrior jumped from a tree and knocked me off the horse," I said lying on my cot talking to Mr. Jeff perched on his hind legs in my hand. "I knew my scalp would be on an Indian's lodge pole before the day was over."

Mr. Jeff twitched his nose continuing to nibble the small piece of cracker.

"Anyway, the Chief Black Buffalo Bull and five other Indians led us back to the shore where Captain Clark, the interpreter Drouillard, and two other men met us in a small boat."

Snooker looked up with interest laying next to the bed listening.

"The interpreter talked to the Chief and finally it was agreed that the Sioux Indians would let us go if we met their conditions. They wanted tobacco, mirrors, beads, grain and Captain Clark's deer skin jacket. But, the thing that really got us out of the tight spot was Captain Clark's bright red hair. The Indians loved it. They called him Chief Fire Hair."

Mr. Jeff cocked his head to one side as though he were thinking over what I had told him.

I looked to a dark corner of the room. A pair of bright eyes stared out of the darkness. Before I could think, the big gray cat howled and pounced on the bed, its claws extended, its mouth wide open showing the rows of deadly sharp teeth. I tossed Mr. Jeff aside. With the other hand I grabbed the cat's tail and hurled him across the room. The cat yowled and raced for the door. Mr. Jeff had already run for safety to the deck.

Mr. Jeff had come within inches of losing his life. I knew I would have to do something very soon or Mr. Jeff would be killed by the large gray beast.

Chapter 10

I poured the syrupy frosting over a flat, two-inch thick cake. Teddy and I worked for hours on the feast. While the men were hunting, repairing the keelboat, cleaning rifles, inventorying the supplies, Teddy and I had been busy with the dinner. Everyone was looking forward to the evening. On shore, over an open fire, we roasted five prairie chickens, baked four loaves of bread, warmed two pots of portable soup, and baked three large flat cakes, covering them with a thick syrup. All the men, including Captains Lewis and Clark, could hardly wait for the meal. It had been weeks since they had eaten so well.

Teddy squatted near the fire stirring the soup. His arm rotated slowly and his eyes were closed.

The old soldier had been up before dawn getting ready for the feast. The Captains told everyone they could take a holiday tonight and be rewarded for their splendid performance so far on the trek. They promised each person an extra dollar to show the President's appreciation for a job well done so far. Privates earned five dollars a month. Corporals earned six dollars a month. A whole dollar seemed almost too much money to hope for all at one time, I thought.

Clearing my throat, I continued rotating a prairie chicken on a spit. Teddy's eyes opened and he looked around as if he were afraid someone might catch him napping.

"Teddy," I said, "why don't you go in and lie down for a while."

The old man's eyes flared angrily. "Don't give me orders, boy! I can outwork a young whippersnapper like you. I've been an army cook for twenty-eight years!"

"I only meant we've got everything under control. A little nap before the men get back wouldn't hurt. Nobody would blame you."

Teddy's voice softened. "I didn't mean to come at you like a wild grizzly, boy. I know you mean well." He shook his head. "It's just that I want to hold my own on this trip."

"Nobody works harder than you. You deserve some time off." I smiled. "I had some time off the other day myself."

The old man lay his head back and laughed. "You did at that, boy. And in one afternoon you caused more trouble than ten boys."

I nodded my head. It was funny to me now that I was back safely.

"You've got a tale to tell your grandchildren, that's for sure," Teddy said, pulling his beard with delight.

"At the time I wasn't sure if I'd ever have any grandchildren. I thought my scalp would be decorating some Sioux's lodge pole before nightfall."

"You handled yourself like a real man, Davey. Even Sergeant Riley was impressed, I'd wager."

I shook my head. "I don't think he'd be impressed if I'd conquer the entire Sioux nation single handed."

"You've done real good, lad."

"I feel lucky to go on an expedition like this."

"Yes, lad. This is a chance of a lifetime. We'll have plenty of tales to tell if we make it back."

I looked up startled. "What do you mean if we make it back?"

Teddy nudged the corner of his mouth with a knuckle. "Of course we'll get back."

I held up my hand. "Wait a minute. I want you to explain. Why shouldn't we make it back?"

Teddy poured the soup into another kettle and covered it with a lid. "You know as much about it as I do. Both the Captains warned us that this was a dangerous journey."

I thought back to the warnings Captain Lewis and Captain Clark gave me in the hotel room that night over three months ago.

"You know we've been lucky so far. We've only had one small run in with Indians. The Tetons, Mandans, Kansas, and Kickapoos have been peaceful. We're taking chances pushing our way down this river...their river."

"But the United States government owns this land now. We've got a document to prove it."

"That document doesn't mean spit to those Indians. And why should it? They've lived here for generations. They raised their children and buried their dead on these lands and shores. They have past and present honorable Chieftains who proudly rule. There are young braves who want to show their manhood by holding on to this land." He shook his head. "No, we've been lucky. To tell you the truth, I can't believe they've let us come this far."

I swallowed, saying nothing.

"And we've still got a winter to go through. It can be very hard to go through a winter in the wilderness. You've got to fight the blustery weather as well as worry about having shelter and enough to eat."

A lump formed in my throat.

"And then there's danger of wild animals. Wolves and maybe bears. Sometimes a wolf pack will get so starved they will circle a man waiting to make their move. And grizzly bears will come at you at times. They are real cantankerous beasts. They are big and clumsy but don't let that fool you. You better not try to outrun them.They'll get you every time. If they stand on their hind legs that means they're just curious and you don't have to worry. But if they come down on all fours and start toward you, you'd better git and git fast." He gestured. "Climb a tree. They won't climb trees after you."

Looking over my shoulder at a wooded area bordering the river, I shivered.

"And there's accidents. This is a dangerous mission. Gun powder could blow up and raise everybody to Kingdom Come. Muskets or rifles may backfire. A lot of things could happen. There's also a chance of getting sick. We've been real lucky. We've had a little dysentary, colds, bug bites, and a few boils. We could catch a disease from the trappers we meet or even some strange disease from the Indians and die overnight." He shook his head. "You just don't know."

A feeling of despair came over me.

Teddy grinned. "Don't worry, lad. We may sail right through all of this without a scratch and get back safe and sound."

He jostled my shoulder.

I shrugged. "Well, I know there are a lot of dangers we've got to overcome. Captains Lewis and Clark told me about them before we started. But, I've got to get back. I...I promised someone I'd get back sure." I bit the tip of my tongue and my face reddened.

Teddy laughed. "Ah, lad, you've got a young lady back there in St. Louis. Is that right?"

Looking away, I shrugged again.

"That's nothing to be ashamed of, lad. A pretty girl will make any man or boy try to survive just that much more." He patted my shoulder. "What's her name by the way?"

"Her name's Priscilla James, but everyone calls her Prissy."

"Prissy...That's a real nice name. I'll bet she's just as pretty as her name."

I nodded. "She is at that. I've got a picture of her if you'd like to see it."

"I'd be right proud to see it," Teddy answered eagerly.

Digging into my pocket, I pulled out the gold locket wrapped in a handkerchief.

Teddy wiped his hands on his breeches and reached for the locket and opened it carefully. He whistled softly.

72

"Oh, now...what a beautiful young lady. I can see why you want to return safe to such a pretty miss."

She is pretty and more. She has the nicest smile and her eyes get all bright when she's happy."

Carefully, I wrapped my handkerchief around the locket and placed it back into my pocket.

"I tell Mr. Jeff all about her at nights," I said shyly.

"Speaking of your Mr. Jeff, yesterday, I walked over half an hour aboard the keelboat before seeing a rat. That big cat of Sergeant Riley's has about got them gone. Your Mr. Jeff better watch his step. Pretty soon the rat population aboard the boats will be down to one and that one will be your pet."

I nodded sadly. "I know, Teddy. I'm getting real worried. I keep him under the bread bin most of the time when I can't keep an eye on him."

Teddy sighed and looked up just as the hunting party broke through the trees on their way back to camp. "Well, we'd better get these victuals on board. It looks like the men are returning and the fun will be beginning real soon."

Private Cruzatte sawed furiously on his fiddle. His bow flew over the strings. I was persuaded to dance for the men. Shuffling and raising my feet high, I danced just the way I did back on the farm in Missouri when Pa played his fiddle. The men laughed and clapped their hands. Everyone had eaten the huge meal. The whiskey cask was opened and dipper after dipper had been drawn from the spigot. Sweat poured down my face as the fiddle wound down. Walking back to a wooden crate, I sat down.

The rest of the men got up. Half of them tied a handkerchief around their left arms playing the "follower" or the woman's part. The "followers" had their arms placed in the crook of the men's arms and they danced around and around not following any particular step or pattern. Loud "hoo-has" and shrill shouts broke the night stillness. The celebration went on and on until the early hours of the morning.

My head dropped wearily on my chest.

"Well, lad, how're you enjoying the party?"

I looked up. Sergeant Riley grinned down at me.

"Fine, Sergeant." I said eyeing him suspiciously.

"You won't think it's so fine when you have to get up in two hours and go back to work," he said drunkenly. "I want you to chop and stack a cord of wood tomorrow. I want you and Cookie to skin and cut up that bear we brought in today. I want you to mend the sail that's ripped in a dozen places. I want fresh water put into all the water casks." He thought for a few moments. "And I want you to air all of the men's bedding and boil the eating utensils." He looked down, his eyes narrowed. "Do you understand, Hutchins?"

I smelled the whiskey on his breath. "Yes, sir. I'll get right to it."

Reaching out, he grabbed me by the collar and pulled me back into the darkness where the firelight was blotted out. His shadow loomed huge. His words slurred.

"You think you're pretty smart don't you, you wet-nosed pup?"

His thick beard tickled my nose as he leaned down looking into my face.

"You've showed me up so far and I don't like it. You've done everything I've told you and haven't complained once. I'll break you yet. They'll see you whining and begging for rest," he said with a look of warning in his eyes.

He released me and tipped the dipper to his lips. He started to walk back to the party swaying dangerously from side to side. Suddenly, he slipped and fell overboard into the Missouri River.

I ran to the edge of the boat. The music and the mens'

shouts were so loud no one heard the splash. Leaning over, I looked down into the water, but saw nothing. Without thinking, I pulled off my boots and dove into the river to search underwater.

I dove beneath the water time and again knowing that if I didn't find him soon it would be too late. Finally, my hand bumped a solid object. He was caught beneath the keelboat and couldn't get loose. I pulled his coat until it tore away from the hull. Bubbles billowed from his mouth and nose. I reached for him, but my hands were batted away. Finally, I grabbed his beard and pulled. Sergeant Riley screamed but it went unheard beneath the water. He followed me unwillingly as I clutched his beard in my fist.

I pulled him to the surface of the water and with all my strength, pushed him over the rail and upon the deck. Weakly, I crawled aboard and rolled him to his stomach pulling his arms above his head. He vomited the river. Finally, he started to cough and moan and I knew he was going to be okay.

Wet and dripping, I shook my head and slowly walked toward my quarters.

Exhausted, I shuffled through the door wanting to get quickly out of my wet clothes. My hand shook from the cold as I lit a candle. Crouched in the opposite side of the room was the big gray cat. Its ears were flattened to its head and the hair bristled on its neck.

Mr. Jeff was backed into a corner. His nose twitched furiously. He stood on his hind legs searching for a means of escape.

I knew there was no way I could reach him in time. The cat was going to win at last, I thought. The cat was much quicker than he was. I closed my eyes.

The cat yowled shrilly jumping straight up. It hissed and looked back over its shoulder. It yowled again as Snooker bit deeper into its tail. Mr. Jeff took the opportunity to race toward the open door. The big cat swung its paws around raking Snooker on the nose. Snooker kept his teeth clamped on the tail. Finally, the cat knew he had met his match and tried to scramble away but Snooker kept its tail locked in his jaws.

I doubled up laughing at the funny sight. "Okay, Snooker, let him go," I said. "Maybe this will teach him a lesson."

Snooker released the cat's tail. It shrieked one last time before it leaped for the door, its feet hardly hitting the floor.

Snooker walked over to me and licked my hand. I checked the raw claw marks on his nose.

"Good boy, Snooker," I said trailing my hand down his back and patting him on the muzzle. "You saved Mr. Jeff for sure." A sadness filtered through me. Even though I knew Mr. Jeff had been saved, he had been very lucky. A few seconds later and he would have been dead. I knew it was time to do something about it.

Chapter 11

Mr. Jeff stood in my palm nibbling a cracker. It had been two days since the incident with the cat. During these two days I thought about the course to take.

The candle flame flickered as cold gusts of wind swept beneath the door. It was late in the year and the water next to the shore was coated in an icy glaze in the mornings. The tree limbs were bare and reached out like naked arms toward the sky. Flocks of geese headed south in precise formations.

"I hope you understand, Mr. Jeff," I said. "It's the only thing to do." Reaching out, I brushed my finger over the little white spot on the rat's head. "Almost every rat on the boat has been killed. You had a close call." I looked down at Snooker and smiled. "If it hadn't been for Snooker you'd be a memory right now. Next time Snooker or I may not be around. You can't stay under the bread bin all the time."

Mr. Jeff stopped nibbling the cracker. His black eyes stared at me quizzically.

"This is for your own good." I patted him on the forehead once again. "I want you to find a warm place. The snow is going to start flying in a short time."

I think Mr. Jeff understood that tonight was not like the many other nights I talked about the farm, Ma and Pa, St. Louis, and Prissy. Tonight, I wasn't smiling.

Sighing, I reached down and rubbed Snooker. "Well, Snooker, I suppose it's time. I'm sure everybody has gone to sleep except the sentry and he's on the bow. We won't be seen if we're real quiet."

Snooker looked up and whined.

Blowing out the candle, I got to my feet. "Okay," I said quietly, "let's go." I placed Mr. Jeff on my shoulder and walked toward the door with Snooker at my heels.

The door creaked open and I held my breath. Looking both ways, I walked out on the deck. The wind swept over me and I shivered. The keelboat was anchored forty yards from shore. I heard the water lap at the bottom of the hull. The buzzing of snoring came from the sleeping quarters. The sentry's heels clicked as he paced back and forth on the bow.

I walked to the side of the boat. The board was where I left it this morning when I was sure my decision was final. I pulled it from an unused crate and tried it several times before tieing a rope to it and dropping it over the side to be sure it would float. I made a mast and rigged a sail. Mr. Jeff, I told myself, was going to leave in style.

Kneeling on the deck, I picked Mr. Jeff off my shoulder. "Well, Mr. Jeff," I whispered, "I guess this is goodbye. You'll be fine when you reach shore." I petted his head. "I'll never forget you even when the journey is over." Carefully, I placed him on the board and lifted it over the side setting it easily on the surface of the water. Snooker raised up on his hind legs to peer into the water. Mr. Jeff scampered back and forth on the board in fright as it started to move away from the boat.

The wind caught the sail and whisked it smoothly down stream. In a matter of moments the tiny craft was far away from the boat. As I lost sight of it in the darkness, a lump as big as a fist lodged in my throat.

"He'll be all right, Snooker," I said struggling to speak. "Mr. Jeff is a smart rat. He'll make it to shore."

Snooker whined helplessly. I brushed the back of my hand beneath my drooling nose as Snooker and I walked back to our sleeping quarters.

Chapter 12

At last our little party could go no further. Ice was starting to form on the river. Captains Lewis and Clark decided the expedition must halt and make winter camp. We would continue up the Missouri in the spring.

They decided to build our winter camp among the Mandan villages; thus the name Fort Mandan. The Mandan Indians welcomed us because they were surrounded by the hostile Sioux. The white men could help them fight if the Sioux attacked. At that point we had traveled 1,600 miles into the wilderness.

The Mandans numbered four hundred people and occupied five villages near the mouth of the Knife River. Here the great Missouri made a big sweep to the west.

The "fort" was a triangular structure, open on top, the two long fences measuring eighteen feet on the outside, the third fence was little more than a gate. It was constructed of cottonwood logs notched at the ends and "dobbed" together with mud at the cracks. The fireplaces were made of stone. It was a poor excuse for a fort but its eighteen foot walls would stop a Sioux attack.

I worked long hours helping build the fort. Sergeant Riley followed me ordering me to work faster and harder. At night, when I pulled the buffalo blankets up beneath my chin, every bone in my body ached.

Once the fort was built, the supplies secured and ready for winter, and the boats safely put in dry-dock, I had time to get to know the Mandan people. I discovered they were happy people who grinned and laughed a lot. There was an unusually large number of chiefs in each village. Every male above the age of twenty-one claimed to be some kind of chief. I was allowed to sit with the "chiefs" while they smoked their pipes.

Private Cruzatte entertained with his fiddle in the evenings. The men and the Mandans danced to the music until they fell to the ground exhausted. Even though languages separated us, the Indians were fast becoming our friends.

Captain Lewis brought his Harrison air gun with him on the trip. The Mandans marveled over the gun, watching birds fall from the sky with no more than a muffled bang.

The crew showed the Mandans how to make a gristmill to grind their maize and wheat into flour. This invention was left with them and would help them for years to come.

A forge was built on the keelboat. The billows frightened the Indians at first, but later fascinated them. They called the white-hot forge "big medicine." They'd squat beside it for hours watching it.

Our Indian friends helped us with the food supply. The tribe hunted buffalo from horseback. Sometimes a brave Mandan youth would go on foot wrapped in a buffalo robe carrying a head of a buffalo on a stick. He'd coax the leaders to follow him and then duck behind a rock near a cliff. Many of the beasts followed him and tumbled to their deaths.

Much of the buffalo meat was smoked and stored away for winter. The skins were made into moccasins, robes and blankets.

This was my first buffalo hunt and I was very excited. Stopping my horse on a knoll, I looked into the distance. My breath caught at the spectacle below. It looked like a huge black cloud had settled on the ground. The "cloud" milled internally.

The horse snorted eagerly. I reached forward, patting

its silken neck. The bright November sun reflected off the red-gold coat. The air was sharp and crisp and swooped across my face.

The black cloud stretched as far as my eyes could see. I couldn't believe there were this many buffalo in the whole world.

Looking back, I saw the five braves following me. My special friend, Black Fox, was right behind me. Black Fox motioned to go forward slowly. We didn't want to frighten the herd while they were still so far away.

After a slow, even pace, I saw the distinct outlines of the buffalo ahead. Some of them on the outside of the herd raised their heads and snorted in our direction. Gusts of cold mist burst from their flared nostrils. Small calves huddled close to their mothers. Mammoth bulls pawed the ground nervously. Buffalo, laying in the sun, rose to their feet and stood with watchful eyes.

One of the leaders reared his head and bellowed. The deep, hollow sound echoed from the hills in the distance.

We sat poised on our mounts ready for the chase. The calves bawled with fright, pushing their way into the middle of the herd.

Black Fox screamed and poked his heels into his pinto's flanks. The horse charged forward. The Mandan braves and I followed his dust-filled trail.

I searched for the right animal. Not twenty yards to my left a bull moved from the interior of the circle. The huge head and full mane were impressive. The bull's small glassy eyes rolled with fear.

I knew that in order for us to survive the winter many buffalo had to be killed. I always regretted downing such a noble beast.

Biting my lip, I wheeled the horse sharply to the left and the chase began. Since starting the trek, I had become a skilled rider and raised up off the horse like the Mandans.

The thick dust turned day into night. Sounds of thousands of thundering hooves beat into my ears. Shrill shrieks of the Indians went unheard beneath the thunder of the hoofbeats.

The bull saw me coming for him and pivoted back trying to get into the middle of the herd. He was blocked by the other bodies. Moving away from the herd, he went on his own.

I couldn't believe the speed of such a huge animal. Standing, it looked awkward with its spindly legs supporting such a large body. But when needed, it ran like a deer.

My hands tightened around the reins as I flew through the wind. The chase went on for several minutes. Grunts of exertion came from the horse. The bull kept on running, lather gathering at his mouth. The horse was wet with sweat and lathered as well. The hooves thundered behind me.

The bull's tiny eyes glistened with dread knowing its fate. Bringing up my rifle, I aimed. The first shot failed to slow the huge beast. I shot once more. This time it was well-placed, and the beast stumbled forward and went down. It rolled to its side.

Reining in my horse, I had a mixture of feelings. I felt victorious and knew I would bring home meat and skins that were much needed, but I also felt sorrow that such a noble animal had to die.

On March third ducks passed over the river. It was time to prepare to leave. Rifles were cleaned and their locks regulated. The swivel guns were put in order. Provisions were stockpiled and inspected. Blankets were aired. On March twenty-third we departed. It was time to travel on and explore the vast region up river.

The party was to leave with two added people. The French interpreter, Charbonneau, insisted on bringing his wife and baby with us this time. The baby had been born at the fort on February eleventh. The mother of the child's name was Sacajawea, which means Bird-Woman in Snake Indian language. The baby was a boy named Baptiste. Captains Lewis and Clark didn't like the idea of taking a woman and a baby on such a dangerous trip. But she was a Snake Indian and spoke Shoshonean. This ability would be valuable in the country we were approaching.

On April seventh we sent the keelboat back down river with eight men to deliver the diaries, stuffed animals, and other specimens to President Jefferson.

The rest of us went up the Missouri from Fort Mandan on the two flat bottom boats and six canoes. It was five o'clock in the afternoon on a cool, clear day. Snooker sat quietly in my lap while I paddled.

Choking back the sadness I felt, I waved my final good-bye to my good friend, Black Fox.

Chapter 13

The mighty Missouri turned cruel as we went up river. Many times it was so shallow our crew had to get out and push in water as cold as ice. My teeth chattered pushing the boat with all my strength. The bottom of the river was muddy in places and we sank to our knees or it was so rocky it cut through our moccasins. Our store bought boots had worn out long ago.

There were still days when the snow flew and the wind cut us like daggers. We encountered hordes of blood-thirsty mosquitoes and saw huge lumbersome grizzlies plodding along the shore. There was one pest particularly nasty. It was a blowfly that landed on our backs, shoulders, or eyes and stung furiously. These flies were so big that we named them buffalo gnats.

Our party was called to a halt on June fourth when we came to a great fork in the river. Which was the Missouri? No one knew. The river on the right was muddy like the Missouri and meandered northward. The fork on the left wound southward. It was clear and clean with a smooth bottom suggesting it came from the faraway mountains.

Captains Lewis and Clark decided to make camp at the fork until a decision was made. The next morning Captain Lewis took a small party of men and went up the north fork while Captain Clark and a few men went the southern route.

Captain Lewis traveled sixty miles up the northern fork before deciding it was not the Missouri. Clark and his party were convinced their route was indeed the Missouri. They saw the snow-capped Rocky Mountains in the distance.

Getting game was no problem this far up river. The

animals had never seen white men nor their guns. They stood quietly and waited.

There were signs along the banks that Indians were in this section of the river. We found smouldering campfires, moccasins, and Indian tools along the banks. We had not seen an Indian, however, since leaving Fort Mandan. This worried us. We feared an ambush or an outright war. Captains Lewis and Clark knew that an ambush, even if we were to survive, would mean we would have to turn back.

"Step lively, lad. We can't take all day!" the Sergeant screamed.

Adjusting the heavy, bulky pack on my back, I nodded.

"Maybe it's too rough for you, Hutchins," he sneered. "It takes men to go on a hunt."

The leather straps sliced into my shoulders. Salty sweat ran down my forehead and burned my eyes. Sergeant Riley had piled most of the camping equipment on my back.

I licked my upper lip. "I'll try to walk faster, Sergeant."

"You wanted to come on this hunt didn't you, Hutchins? Maybe you're not man enough to go on a hunt yet. Could that be it?" he asked, throwing his head back laughing.

A spread of hot anger prickled my scalp. "No, sir," I replied. "I want to go on this hunt." I quickened my pace. "I'll keep up with you." Pulling a handkerchief from my pocket, I wiped the sweat from my face.

"Why don't you let me help you carry some of that, Davey? You don't have to prove anything to anyone. The Sergeant's been riding you ever since we left St. Charles," Tandy said.

I glanced up at Corporal Tandy. I liked the smooth-faced eighteen-year-old. Tandy had always been fair to me.

"Thanks. But, I'm not going to let him beat me. I've put up with him for months and I can put up with him for a few more."

Corporal Tandy shook his head. "Why is he after your hide, anyway?" He moved his rifle to the opposite shoulder.

I shrugged. "Oh, it started back in St. Louis when I tried to sign on the expedition. I went behind his back."

"Is that the whole thing?" Tandy asked.

I looked down at Snooker. "Well, Snooker bit him on the leg the morning we left when he tried to rough me up a bit. And then he got mad when Captain Clark countermanded his orders and let me ride the roan." I grinned.

"What are you grinning about? With that pack on your back I don't know how you could feel that good," Corporal Tandy said looking at me.

I hunched my shoulders. "It has to do with the rats and that big gray cat of Sergeant Riley's. I think he thought he had me on that one."

"What happened? All I know is that beast has cleaned up every rat aboard the boats."

"Every rat but one," I said slyly thinking back to Mr. Jeff's midnight escape.

"What are you talking about? We haven't seen a rat on board for weeks now."

"I know," I said still smiling.

Sergeant Riley turned and put his hand in the air calling for a halt. "We're going to split up here." He gestured. "I want everybody but Hutchins to go with Corporal Tandy to the north."

I shifted my feet uneasily.

Tandy looked at me. "Sergeant, sir," he said, "we're only a few men here. Maybe we should all go together."

"Are you doubting my orders, Corporal Tandy?" he

asked. "I've been in the army for twenty-four years and you barely two."

Tandy shook his head. "No, sir, it's not that. I only think we should stay together."

"What is it, Tandy? Are you Hutchins' nursemaid or something?"

I bit into my lip trying to control my anger.

"No, sir. As far as I'm concerned, Davey can take care of himself. I think he's proved it so far on this trip."

The Sergeant waved his hand. "I said we're splitting up and split up we will. Now, if you don't like the idea, I can put someone else in charge and you can go back to camp." He stared at the Corporal waiting for his reply.

Corporal Tandy looked at me.

"All right, Sergeant Riley," he said. "When do you want us to get back and meet?"

"That's using good sense, Corporal." He grinned. "We will meet back here in four hours. By that time it'll be getting close to dusk. If you kill anything too big, mark it and we'll get some help later. Is that understood?"

The men nodded their heads.

Corporal Tandy picked up his rifle and turned to me. "Good luck Davey," he said.

"Thanks, Corporal."

Tandy pressed my shoulder and signaled for his men to follow him in a northern direction.

I watched the men leave shuffling through the carpet of pine needles and zigzagging around trees.

"Well, what are you waiting for, Hutchins?" Sergeant Riley growled. "We're out here to find game not to stand around and gawk." He pulled on his beaver skin hat.

"Yes, sir. Where should we look first?" I pointed. "Maybe we could cut across that open area and look for a grazing deer or antelope."

A scowl came to his face. "You're filled with answers like always, ain't you, lad?"

"I didn't mean it that way," I said. "You're the leader."

Sergeant Riley placed his hands on his hips. "Well, you finally realize that, do you? You don't act like it."

"If I led you to think that, Sergeant, I'm sorry."

Sergeant Riley threw his head back and laughed. "You've got a fine way of showing it. You go over my head. You get my orders countermanded. That dog of yours bit me and made me look foolish the day we started." He paused, his eyes narrowing. "I don't like it, lad. I don't like it at all."

"I didn't mean to do any of those things."

He leaned down. The puckered scar deepened on his face. "All right, Hutchins, now we test you as a hunter. We'll see if you should've come on a man's expedition." Sergeant Riley signaled and trudged forward.

Hefting my heavy pack, I whistled for Snooker to follow. Rabbits, squirrels, prairie chickens, and martens skittered out of our way as we traveled forward.

My knees started to weaken as I struggled up one steep hill after another. The leather straps stung my back and shoulders and after two hours, I dripped with sweat.

On one brief stop, I took out Prissy's locket and looked at her picture. After being in the wilderness all these months and going through all of the trials and adventures, St. Louis seemed like a dream.

"Let's go, Hutchins! This ain't no tea party," the Sergeant shouted. "We've got two more hours to get something."

I called Snooker lapping at a mountain stream.

After a half hour more of pulling ourselves up steep foothills and sliding down embankments, we spotted a lone elk grazing at the bottom of a deep ravine.

Putting up his hand, Sergeant Riley signaled for silence. "I'll bring in this one, Hutchins," he whispered. "You be quiet and keep that dog of yours from yapping and scaring it away." He pulled his rifle from his shoulder.

I stopped, happy to lay the pack down for a few moments.

Sergeant Riley lifted his rifle to his shoulder and took careful aim. Crack! The shot flashed through the hills. The big elk reared back and then looked calmly up at us. Sergeant Riley hurried to reload but his rifle jammed.

The elk wheeled around suddenly realizing the danger. With majestic grace, it bolted forward.

Sergeant Riley continued to work on his rifle. I brought my rifle up and aimed at the fleeing animal. Looking down the barrel, I squeezed the trigger evenly. Blue smoke rose from my gun and the strong smell of gun powder stung my nostrils.

Sergeant Riley looked up seeing the big animal lying on its side, dead. He turned around his face red with rage.

"Why'd you do that, Hutchins? Who gave you orders to shoot that elk?"

"I...I just thought..." I stammered helplessly.

"Who told you to think?" he shouted, pointing his finger. "You don't think. You take orders like everyone else!"

"I thought by the time you got your rifle ready the elk would be far away. What does it matter who shoots it?" I added.

Charging toward me, he grabbed my shoulers. The scar on his face deepened. His bearded chin jutted forward.

My eyes grew large. Snooker crowded next to me baring his teeth in a warning growl.

"You did it to show me up again, Hutchins! You did it deliberately so the men would laugh when we reported that the only game brought back was shot by you!" he shouted.

"I didn't mean anything like that. The elk would've gotten away," I explained feebly.

"Then let it get away! I didn't tell you to shoot. You take orders from me just like the rest of the men. Do you understand?"

Snooker lunged forward snapping his teeth at him. He kicked at Snooker furiously.

"I'll get rid of that dog someday," he shouted. "I'll get rid of him just like I got rid of those pesky rats aboard the keelboat."

I started to reply but my attention was changed to the lifeless elk below.

Sergeant Riley turned to look.

A grizzly bear cub ran out of a clump of bushes preparing for an unexpected meal. It romped playfully up to the dead carcass and sniffed it.

The Sergeant smiled. "Well, look what we have here. The men would like a pet like that to play with during the long days ahead." Without a word, he threw his rifle aside and raced down the slope to capture the cub.

Cupping my hands to my mouth, I called out a warning.

Sergeant Riley chased the cub one direction and then another. Finally, he grabbed a hind leg and lifted it into his arms. The little creature wiggled and snarled trying to free itself.

He lifted his fist in a sign of victory. Holding the cub in his arms, he started up the steep ravine. A roar vibrated the ground beneath our feet. Sergeant Riley froze in his tracks turning to see the huge mother of the grizzly cub. She was walking on her hind legs toward him. Her mouth was wide open and her sharp fangs flashed in the sunlight.

Sergeant Riley dropped the cub hoping that its release would satisfy her. The cub paused curiously for a few moments and then scampered back to its mother.

I hoped the mother and baby would disappear into the trees now that she was satisfied having him back, but she kept advancing toward Sergeant Riley, roaring with anger.

Mouth open and unable to move, Sergeant Riley looked at the huge beast. Snooker lunged forward barking. I caught the back of his neck and held on tight.

93

The bear dropped down on all fours and charged. I gulped remembering what Teddy had told me months ago.

Sergeant Riley's wits returned and he started to scramble up the ravine, slipping and sliding on loose rock. The bear was only yards from him.

Snooker tore away from my hold and scampered down the ravine. I reached for him, but he was gone. Grabbing my rifle, I hurried after him.

Snooker barked and the bear's attention was briefly steered away from the Sergeant. Snooker yipped and yapped at the bear's legs, pulling out small tufts of hair. The bear snarled with fury.

The grizzly stopped only feet from Sergeant Riley and lunged at Snooker. Snooker reared back each time the mighty jaws snapped shut.

Sergeant Riley raced for a nearby tree. I had never seen a man scramble up a tree faster in my life.

The bear stopped its charge and swiped at Snooker with its huge paws. I gasped as Snooker was thrown back by the mighty paw. He lay there whimpering for a moment and then jumped up charging the bear again. Blood streamed down his flank.

"Snooker! Snooker, boy! Come on back!" I yelled.

Snooker charged the bear again and again. A yipe was heard as a paw hit him throwing him high into the air. He landed ten yards away. This time he didn't get up.

I screamed, waving my rifle as the bear bolted forward to finish him off. Aiming my rifle, I fired. The grizzly roared and lurched to its hind legs. It looked in my direction showing a mouth filled with deadly fangs.

I hurriedly started to reload. The bear suddenly pivoted and ran into the trees, its cub following at its heels.

My heart pounded in my chest. I raced down the ravine toward Snooker, slipping and falling.

Laying down my rifle, I dropped beside him. Blood was spattered over Snooker's body. A claw had ripped a deep gash in his side. His breathing heaved in and out as he whimpered in pain.

"Snooker!" I shouted. "Don't die, boy. Please, don't die."

Picking him up in my arms, I stumbled back up the ravine toward camp. I didn't wait for Sergeant Riley's orders this time.

Chapter 14

Sacajawea, with baby Baptiste in a cradle on her back, took Snooker from my arms. She went right to work.

I sat there with Teddy watching the woman's careful hands. Laying Snooker carefully on a buffalo blanket, she heated a pot of water until it steamed. She took a cloth and bathed Snooker's torn flesh.

Next, she soaked a cloth with whiskey to kill the infection. She made a poltice out of herbs to suck out whatever infection was there. Last of all, she threaded a thin piece of rawhide into a bone needle and sewed the deep gash together.

Her long, brown fingers worked nimbly as Snooker's head lay in my lap. I watched her sew the two flaps of flesh together, noticing how they met perfectly.

The men and Sergeant Riley had returned hours ago. They were having supper at the far end of the camp. Sergeant Riley was unusually quiet tonight.

Snooker breathed more regularly. He lapped up a little water and then went back to sleep. Sacajawea snipped the rawhide thread and examined her work. Baby Baptiste gurgled with pleasure on her back.

Looking down into my lap, I saw the rise and fall of Snooker's side as he slept.

"Most dogs don't make it when a grizzly gets hold of 'em. That makes Snooker even more special, Davey, lad," Teddy said with a smile.

Nodding, I smoothed the hair on one of Snooker's ears.

Teddy got to his feet and stretched. "Well, I'd better get back and see if the men are getting fed proper-like. I hear them grumbling from here." Teddy patted me on the shoulder, swiped beneath his nose, and stiffly walked to the far end of the camp to see to the mens' supper.

A knot of sorrow lodged in my throat. What if Snooker didn't make it? He had lost a lot of blood, I thought. Infection could set in and then there would be little hope.

"How's he doing, Hutchins?"

My eyes blinked in the darkness trying to see beyond the campfire. Red-hot tongues of flame licked into the night revealing the bushy face of Sergeant Riley.

Saying nothing, I looked down at Snooker.

Sergeant Riley walked into the light of the fire. He looked at Snooker sleeping peacefully but for an occasional whimper of pain.

"I just came over to see how the dog was doing. I wasn't hungry tonight," he said nervously.

"Sacajewea cleaned the wound and sewed him up. It's too early to tell how he'll be. He's lost a lot of blood."

"He's a spunky critter, I'll say that for him," Sergeant Riley said, bending low to look at him.

"Snooker's the best dog a guy could have. Pa got him for me five years ago."

"I"ve never seen a braver dog, that's for sure," he said petting Snooker along the muzzle.

Sergeant Riley sat crosslegged beside me. He spat and cleared his throat. Finally, he pulled off his beaver skin hat and laid it in his lap.

"I think it's time I did some apologizing, lad," he said looking straight into my eyes.

I remained silent.

"All these months I've ridden you day and night. I've given you the worst chores I could find. I've worked you twice as hard as any of the other men."

"You don't have to say all this."

Sergeant Riley shook his head. "Don't shush me up now, boy. It's taken me all evening to get the guts to come over here and tell you this. A brush with death makes a man want to right things. If it wasn't for you and your dog I'd be chewed to the bone by the biggest bear this side of the Missouri." He raked his fingers through his beard. "You've saved my life, lad." He shook his head. "I'm a small man compared to you, Davey Hutchins," he said, his voice quivering.

I shook my head. "I just want us to get along the rest of the time on this expedition."

"In fact, you've saved my life twice," he said.

I looked up.

"Corporal Tandy saw the whole thing that night you saved my sorry hide when I fell overboard. He told me tonight at supper."

Sergeant Riley suddenly got to his feet and shouted to the men in the distance finishing their supper. "Men! Men! All of you! Come here!"

The men crowded around the campfire with the Sergeant, Snooker, and me in the center of a human semi-circle.

"My pardons, Captain Lewis and Captain Clark. I didn't mean to order the both of you here, too."

"Never mind that, Sergeant Riley. This is the wilderness and a thousand miles from any sign of civilization. Some of the decorum of the military doesn't have its place here as it should be," Captain Clark said.

"Thank you both, Captains," Sergeant Riley said cordially.

Captain Clark's brows arched in doubt. "Would this have anything to do with Hutchins and his dog, Sergeant Riley?"

"I've got a confession tonight," he said. "I want to tell all of you in the presence of Davey and his dog what a terrible man I've been. Today was the last straw. I came close to meeting my Maker. It all started months ago at the Parker Hotel in St. Louis when Davey tried to sign up for the trip." He shook his head. "He begged me to let him go.

I'm ashamed to say I threw him down in the dirt and told him to get out."

Teddy looked at Tandy and winked.

"Well, that didn't discourage Hutchins. He used his brains. He climbed a ladder to Captain Lewis and Captain Clark's hotel room window." He smiled and tugged his beard. "I hear tell the ladder slipped away and left him dangling by his fingernails."

The men laughed and elbowed one another.

The Sergeant continued. "When I found Davey had somehow gotten permission to go on the expedition, I was mad and vowed to get back at him for going over my head. I did everything to make his life miserable. Of course Captain Lewis and Captain Clark didn't know this or they'd have my hide. When my orders were countermanded, I blamed it on him and rode him harder." He hung his head shamefully once again. "Today was the last straw. This lad and his dog have saved my miserable hide not once but two times on this expedition." He paused and scratched his hairy chin. "Today his dog saved my life by fighting a grizzly that just about had me by the tail."

Every eye turned and looked at me.

"He's the one who bagged the elk after I missed it today." The Sergeant bowed his head.

Captain Lewis looked sternly at Sergeant Riley. "If we had known any of this was going on Sergeant, we would have stepped in and the matter would have been at an end."

"No, sir. Davey didn't want the men to say anything," Teddy replied from the crowd.

"The point is," Captain Lewis continued, "Sergeant Riley knows better. He had no right to take matters in his hands. This could be a matter for a court martial."

"Just a minute, sir," I said raising my hand. "If it's all right with you, I would just as soon forget it and go on from here." I looked at Sergeant Riley. "I think Sergeant

100

Riley is a good soldier. I would hate to lose his leadership."

Captain Lewis shrugged and turned to Captain Clark. They talked in hushed tones. Sergeant Riley stood before them wringing his hat nervously in his hands.

Finally, Captain Clark cleared his throat. "Captain Lewis and I agree with Davey. We need hard work and cooperation from everyone. If Davey is willing to forgive you, Sergeant, then so can we. But, we must warn you that you will be watched closely and if we see that your conduct falls back to the way it was, you're in trouble."

Sergeant Riley nodded his head. "Thank you, sirs. You don't have to worry about me." He measured with his fingers. "When your behind comes a wee piece away from the jaws of a man-eating grizzly, you take stock of yourself." He extended his hand to me.

The men shouted and tossed their hats into the air. Captain Lewis and Captain Clark stepped forward and shook my hand as well.

I looked down and Snooker's eyes were wide open. He licked my hand. I knew then that he was going to be all right.

Chapter 15

In a few days Snooker was better. He couldn't run but walked stiffly favoring his left hind leg. This leg would always remain weak and carried a couple of inches off the ground for the rest of his life.

Sacajawea examined him daily. She searched beneath the hair for signs of infection. She kept the wound clean and carefully wrapped. By sign language, she cautioned me to keep him still during his recovery.

Sergeant Riley came to see Snooker every day. He brought him choice parts of meat after a hunt. One day, he even made a braided rope collar for him.

###

Our party camped at the foothills of the Rocky Mountains. The jagged, snow-capped peaks stared down on us. Even though it was late summer we discovered cold weather comes early in the mountains. On the first week in September, the camp woke up to six inches of snow. The world was covered in a blanket of white as far as the eye could see. This was only our first surprise. We also woke up finding ourselves completely surrounded by a band of Indians. The Indians stood like statues holding tomahawks. Their arrows were drawn. Some held old muskets. They had war-paint streaked across their faces.

I held Snooker back by his rope collar. Every man in camp stood by his tent rubbing his eyes hoping it was only a bad dream.

Captain Clark trudged through the ankle-deep snow all humor absent in his face. Captain Lewis joined him trying to look the picture of calm. They realized one inappropriate word or one wrong move could start a battle. A battle we would most likely lose.

Captain Lewis pulled the buffalo blanket from his shoulders, being sure his hands were not concealed. Captain Clark doffed his hat revealing his bright hair. Unfortunately, it seemed to have little effect this time. Their brown, leathery faces revealed no trace of emotion.

Captain Clark stood before their leader. He twirled a blanket over his head and intermittently laid it on the ground. Sacajawea had told him this was the sign for "friend".

Captain Lewis repeated the word "Tabba-bone" over and over again. This word merely meant, strangers. There was no word for white men.

The leader stepped forward. Bright pheasant feathers adorned his shoulder-length black hair. His shoulders were massive and his waist narrow. Corded muscles bulged from a brief deer-skin vest. His face was streaked with red berry dye.

Charbonneau stepped forward with the Captains to interpret.

Captain Lewis commenced his usual speech about the territory now belonging to the great white father. Charbonneau translated his words. The Indian leader showed little interest and was visibly unimpressed.

After the speech, Captain Lewis signaled for gifts to be brought out and given to the Indians.

Each time they laid the mirrors, beads, awls, bright cloth, army hats and coats before them, the Chief shook his head and grunted his disapproval.

"What is it, Charbonneau? We've showed him everything. There's nothing left," said Captain Lewis.

"He ees not impressed," Charbonneau said with his thick French accent. "Everytheeng we've shown heem, he shrugs off."

Captain Lewis looked disgruntled. "Tell him we will not

be pushed. Tell him we come as friends to explore this vast territory. We mean no harm to him or the Pawnee Nation. His war paint and drawn weapons do not show good faith on his part."

Charbonneau turned to the leader and relayed Captain Lewis' message.

Chief Long Bow grunted and responded in a few words.

"He reelly does not care about eet. We should not be here according to heem. Thees is the land of his people and his ancestors. We mock eet by coming here."

Captain Clark stepped forward smiling. There was a pallor in his face instead of the usual healthy ruddiness.

"Charbonneau, tell Chief Long Bow we will move on very soon. We come in peace and we want to leave in peace."

The Chief remained sober as he turned to listen to Charbonneau.

"He said that he weel make up his mind what he wants soon. Perhaps, we do have sometheeng that will be of interest. He would like to smoke a pipe and theenk about eet."

Captain Clark grinned generously. "Oh, of course." He bowed and motioned toward his tent.

The Chief looked around the camp at the solemn, cautious faces. His eyes met mine and and we looked at each other for several seconds. Finally, he looked away and walked to Captain Clark's tent.

For two hours the bone pipe was passed from Captain Lewis, to the Chief, to Captain Clark. Little was said during this time. The Chief only nodded or shook his head as Charbonneau continued to try to persuade him to leave the small expedition alone.

Pulling a buffalo blanket up beneath my chin, I looked at the Indians standing with their weapons ready. Not one had changed positions in all this time. Only their eyes moved when a member of our party moved.

I looked up as the tent flap was flung back and the Chief, Captains, and Charbonneau emerged. The leaders looked grim.

Nothing had been settled. So far, it was a stand-off. Would this place, beneath the jagged peaks of the Rocky Mountains, be as far as we would go? I asked myself. We'd be no match for the sixty Pawnee warriors surrounding our camp.

Captain Lewis and Captain Clark talked in hushed tones. Their faces were etched with worry.

The Chief took up his post once again and peered down on the small party of white men.

I looked up at him and discovered he was staring at me again. His dark eyes stayed with me watching my every move.

Captain Clark walked over to Teddy. "Cookie, call the men over to breakfast. We must go ahead with our daily routine. It is their turn to tell us what they want. Until they do, we must go ahead as though we have nothing to fear."

"Right away, Captain," Teddy said hitting a spoon against a pot, calling the men to eat.

The men squatted around the campfire eating sour dough biscuits and bear stew. Their eyes remained on the Indians standing on the knoll surrounding them.

After breakfast, the men sat around the campfire repairing their gear, shaving, washing clothes, talking, or looking suspiciously up at the Indians.

Captain Lewis, with Charbonneau, talked with Chief Long Bow at noon. Lewis came away shaking his head in frustration.

The sun started to dip in the west. It's blaze dimmed as it sank slowly behind a row of snow-capped mountain peaks.

Suddenly, there was movement from the Chief. He shouted in his tongue and the Captains and Charbonneau raced up to him to hear what he had to say.

All the men in camp were standing straight and rigid. Some were holding small crucifixes and silently repeating words of prayer.

The Chief, stern and bold as ever, told Charbonneau his demands. At the end of his booming statement, he pointed. Every man followed his finger which led to me.

Charbonneau turned to Captain Lewis and Captain Clark. A muscle jerked in his jaw with tension. His beaver skin hat was pulled down over his right eye.

"What is it, Charbonneau? What does he want?" Captain Lewis demanded.

"Eet's hard to believe, sir. Chief Long Bow wants nothing to do with our white man's trinkets, as he calls them. He says they are only playthings for squaws, anyway. He ees angry that we offered them to heem."

"So, what does he want? What can we give him to go away and leave us alone?" Clark asked.

Charbonneau paused for a few moments. At last, he turned and pointed down the knoll. "He wants heem. Chief Long Bow wants Davey Hutchins. He will go away and there will be no bloodshed if we give heem the boy. He ees to replace his son who was killed in a battle a few months ago. If we refuse, he will wipe every man out, he claims," Charbonneau said, his voice starting to shake.

"That's out of the question," Captain Clark said angrily. "We will give no man or boy to these Indians. We will all die fighting before we permit this."

"I theek you'd better theenk about it, sir. They are serious and will fight if we do not do what they want. There will be many lives lost."

"They can't seriously believe we will hand over one of our people to them like he was a buffalo blanket or an officer's coat do they? Davey Hutchins is a member of our expedition and will be protected until every man drops," Captain Lewis said emphatically.

"Captain, sir, don't be hasty," Charbonneau said looking warily over his shoulder at the Chief. "We are talking about one boy's life against the rest of us."

Captain Lewis looked at the Indians surrounding them. He licked his lips and turned toward me.

Captain Clark looked at me and closed his eyes for a few moments in dread.

The two Captains motioned me to meet them on the knoll. Puzzled as to what they wanted, I bolted forward.

Teddy caught my shoulder and held me back briefly. "Be careful, Davey, lad. Those Indians are not fooling around. It's taken too long to make up their minds," he said shaking his head. "We may have a full-scale battle here before we're all done today."

I nodded and rushed forward to stand beside the leaders.

Captain Clark placed his hand on my shoulder. "We've got a problem here, Davey," he said solemnly. "It's a strange one." He paused. "We want you to be in on the decision we give Chief Long Bow. And remember, whatever you decide we'll abide by it."

I looked quizzically up at Captain Clark. I still didn't understand any of this.

Captain Lewis, his jaw set and his eyes narrowed, looked down at me. His eyes stared from beneath his fur-lined hat. "Davey, lad, Chief Long Bow has made a decision as to what he wants from us. It doesn't make sense as far as we're concerned."

Looking at the Chief, I met his dark eyes. I noticed they had softened a little.

Captain Lewis continued. "It seems that Chief Long Bow lost a son about your age in battle a few months ago. He wants nothing from us at all as far as the things we've brought along to give to the various tribes of Indians." He hesitated and nervously licked his upper lip. "He...he wants you, Davey. He wants to take you back with him to replace the son he lost in battle."

My mouth dropped open.

"Of course," Captain Lewis continued, "I told Charbonneau to tell him that it was out of the question. You are a member of this party and as such you are protected by the United States Government. We will tell him that the answer is, no!" he said abruptly.

Charbonneau closed his eyes with regret and wiped the sweat from his forehead with his sleeve.

"Captain Lewis is right, Davey. We're one for all and all for one here. If it comes to fighting we'll fight until the last man drops before we give one of our men up," Captain Clark said looking at me.

A lump of gratitude lodged in my throat. I was sure almost every man felt the same way except for Charbonneau. But there was Sacajawea and Baby Baptiste to consider as well.

Captain Lewis turned to Charbonneau. "Tell Chief Long Bow it's no deal."

Charbonneau shook his head trying to understand an honorable man's reasoning. His hands and voice shook as he started to explain to the Chief.

"Wait!" I shouted before Charbonneau got through the first few words.

"I can't let you do this," I said. "This party was sent by the President of the United States. This land we are exploring will double the size of our country. It's got to go on."

"It will, Davey," Captain Clark assured me. "If we fail, others will try and keep right on trying until the Pacific Ocean is reached."

"But, we're not that far away now," I argued. "I don't want it to end here." I shook my head. "I'm not going to let everyone die on my account." I tried to look brave. "When I joined up, I knew there would be hardships and danger. I knew we might not come back."

"What are you saying, Davey?" Captain Lewis asked.

I tried to control my quaking voice. "I say that I've got

to go with him. That way this expedition can go on in peace and finish and no one will lose any blood."

Captain Lewis looked at Captain Clark. Both men were shaken.

"We can't let you do this, Davey," Captain Clark said in an emotional whisper.

"No, lad, it's out of the question," said Captain Lewis.

"Then you're both saying that the expedition is over. You're saying that we've all failed. You've given up for one person." I looked at Captain Lewis.

Captain Lewis sighed and hung his head. Tears welled in Captain Clark's eyes.

Charbonneau looked at the two white leaders. "The Chief ees getting impatient, sirs. What weel I tell heem?"

"Tell him Davey Hutchins will go with them, Charbonneau," Captain Lewis said.

Charbonneau breathed a sigh of relief and relayed the message. For the first time a brief smile came to the face of Chief Long Bow. He raised his hand and motioned for his braves to lower their weapons.

I turned and waded through the snow to my tent to pack. Shaking my head, I didn't feel so brave now. My stomach swirled and I was afraid I was going to be sick. I was going to be Davey Hutchins, the adopted son of Long Bow, Chief of the Pawnee nation.

Chapter 16

Tieing a rawhide thong around the end of my sack of belongings, I sighed. "I guess that's it." I turned and faced my old friend. "I guess this is goodbye, Teddy."

Teddy reached out and pulled me to him. Finally, I pulled away and rushed out of the tent, refusing to look back.

I blinked my eyes to adjust them to the bright, snowy day. The Indians were mounted on the knoll and looked like stone statues. Every man in camp stood when I came out of the tent. Sacajawea, with Baby Baptiste strapped to her back, was standing near her fire. Her expression was sad.

Charbonneau rushed up to Captain Lewis. "Captain, sir, Chief Long Bow says he wants to leave at once. He ees getting impatient."

Captain Lewis looked up with a scowl. "He'll just have to wait. We've got some sad goodbyes to get over with."

I went from one man to another shaking hands. I walked over to Sacajawea; she reached out taking my hand. I chucked Baby Baptiste beneath the chin.

Shaking Corporal Tandy's hand, I noticed he was biting his lower lip trying to contain his emotions.

Looking up into the sad faces of Captain Lewis and Captain Clark, I knew the time had come to leave. Abruptly, I looked around for Sergeant Riley. My eyes swooped over the camp and into the white foothills. I shrugged disappointedly. He was gone. Perhaps, when things got really bad, the Sergeant made himself disappear. Perhaps, he hadn't changed at all, I thought.

At last I walked up the knoll with Snooker following at my heels. Captain Lewis shook my hand with military formality. He wanted to say something but there was nothing left to say. Captain Clark pulled me to him.

Finally, I turned and walked to the Chief feeling a mixture of disbelief and fear. A horse was ready for me to mount. It was a pinto, proud and spirited. Picking up Snooker, I started to mount. Chief Long Bow raised his hand and spoke gruffly. Charbonneau looked at me and then to Snooker.

"Chief Long Bow says you can not breeng your dog weeth you. Eet would only remind you of the white man."

"This is outrageous!" cried Captain Lewis. "This is the boy's dog. You can't make him leave this animal behind."

Charbonneau closed his eyes wanting the trouble to end. He grudgingly relayed the message to the Chief.

"The Chief ees regretful, but hees mind ees made up. The boy is to breeng nothing weeth heem to remind heem of the white man's ways. He weel be his son now. The proud son of Chief Long Bow."

I looked at the sad stares of the Captains. Snooker would have to stay. Kneeling down beside him, I ran my hand along his back.

"You stay here, old boy. You be a good dog and don't get into any more skirmishes with bears." A lump formed in my throat. "You help Captain Lewis and Captain Clark get to the Pacific Ocean." I choked. "And...and when you get to the end of the expedition, you think of me, you hear? The whole United States will be as proud of you as they will be the men." I rubbed my cheek along Snooker's muzzle. He swiped his wet tongue along my face.

The horses paced nervously. There was nothing left to do. Nuzzling Snooker one last time, I hurriedly mounted the pony.

My eyes swept over the little camp. Teddy waited by the tent, visoring his eyes. Sacajawea and Baby Baptiste were further down the camp. All of the men stood saluting me. I lifted my hand and saluted back. I searched once more for Sergeant Riley. Captain Lewis and Captain Clark saluted me proudly and held the salute until I dropped my hand.

114

Chief Long Bow turned his horse and motioned for me to do the same. Quickly, I took one last look at the camp and my friends. Snooker barked frantically trying to free himself from Captain Clark's arms.

###

We traveled for hours. The night closed in like a black blanket. The air was brittle cold. No one spoke but followed Chief Long Bow as he slowly trudged through the snow.

I shivered as a wolf howled in the distance. I had always loved the wilderness but this was different. Before, there had been a warm cabin to return to. A cabin filled with mouth-watering smells of homemade breads and frying meats. There were familiar faces who would protect me. Even on the expedition there were the friendly faces of Teddy, Tandy, and the warmth of Snooker. I started to shake and it was all I could do to stay mounted.

At last, Chief Long Bow raised his hand. The Indians dismounted and tended their horses. They found a swift mountain stream and watered the animals. Next, a campfire was built and various braves were instructed to get the food ready. Water was brought up from the stream and passed from one person to another. Dried pemmican was given to everyone. I discovered that even though I was filled with fear, I still was hungry.

Five braves took their places to guard the camp. The other braves pulled pine boughs from the trees to cushion them from the ground and snow. Chief Long Bow motioned for me to do the same. Finally, I had a soft mattress of pine boughs. I moved away from the rest of the braves feeling very much a stranger.

My body sank into the pine boughs. I wished I could fall asleep and awaken and the whole episode would have been a bad dream.

Just before I closed my eyes, I fished out Prissy's locket and held it in my cold hand. Would I ever see her again? Would I ever see another white person again as long as I lived? Or would I be with the Pawnee tribe until the end of my days?

Closing my eyes, I sank into a deep sleep. I had no knowledge of Chief Long Bow placing another buffalo blanket over me to ward off the bitter cold.

Chapter 17

The sun leaked through the pine trees striking my closed eyes. In the back of my mind I heard the movement of feet crunching through the crusted snow. Finally, I lurched to a sitting position, blinking my eyes.

Everywhere I looked I saw Indians with buffalo blankets over their hunched shoulders going about the morning duties. Some were cutting wood for the fire. Others were tending the horses. Others were folding blankets getting ready to break camp.

Twenty yards away from me, a small group of braves were laughing and chasing each other. They knocked one another into the snow and got up laughing. I sat watching them for a time realizing they had fun in much the same way as my friends and I did back in Missouri. Some threw snowballs and some just rolled in the snow like playful children.

I could not see Chief Long Bow. I wondered how far we were from the village. How long would it take to reach it? What would it be like once we did reach it?

With a deep sigh, I got to my feet and started to fold my blanket. A blazing fire reached toward the sky. Several braves huddled around it for warmth, talking and laughing.

Slowly, I walked over to the fire and placed my hands next to the flames. They stared at me curiously. Some talked and laughed and I knew their words were about me. Glancing around, I saw a bright object shining in the morning sun around one of the young brave's neck. Leaning closer, I discovered it was the gold locket Prissy had given me. It must have slipped out of my hand when I fell asleep and was stolen. Hot anger built up inside of me. I had to have that locket back, I told myself. Without it, I knew I would never survive.

I pointed. "You've got something that belongs to me," I cried.

The braves looked at the one called Little Elk. Little Elk had devious, shifting eyes. He was lazy and irresponsible but he was a member of the Pawnee Tribe and must have the support of the braves when faced against a white stranger.

Little Elk looked down at the locket shining around his neck. He threw his head back and laughed and said words in Pawnee. The rest of the braves laughed.

"I want it back. You stole it from me. Give it back!" I ordered.

He fondled the locket mockingly.

"I said I want it back! It doesn't belong to you." Pushing my way through the braves, I stood beside him.

Little Elk sneered and started to walk away. Reaching out, I pulled the locket from his throat. Slowly, he pulled the buffalo blanket from his shoulders. Muscles rippled beneath his deerskin shirt. His black hair hung to his shoulders. His eyes narrowed menacingly.

With a scream that ripped the morning air, he rushed and jumped on me encircling my neck.

I grunted feeling his weight and fell to my knees. Looking over my shoulder, I saw the hating eyes and the clenched teeth.

Every brave rushed from his duties to watch the fight. The adopted white son of Chief Long Bow was battling Little Elk, one of the best fighters in the tribe.

Vaulting back, I fell on top of Little Elk. The braves laughed and shouted, waking the still mountain morning.

My fingers dug beneath the strong grip. But, the months of hard work in the wilderness had also paid off for me and I managed to throw the arm away and bounce to my feet.

Little Elk crouched, his black eyes darting, awaiting an opening. I moved in a low crouch as well, watching every movement.

118

Little Elk dove for my legs and I quickly shifted to one side. The Indian brave flew through the air landing on his face. He looked up, his face coated with snow. Everyone laughed.

I stayed in a low crouch letting him call the moves. Little Elk was eager to get the fight over with.

He lurched forward grappling my shoulders. Reaching out, I clutched his shoulders. The combined weight and strength of both of us toppled us to the ground.

Grappling each other, we started rolling down the steep hill. Over and over we rolled still clinging to each other. The braves hooted and hollered.

High on a bluff, Chief Long Bow watched this match of strength. We continued rolling down the steep embankment finally impacting with a huge boulder. This jolted us to a stop and we lay there wrestling each other for several minutes, neither of us getting the advantage.

I was wet with sweat even though my body was covered with snow. My breath burst in gusts and my muscles ached.

Little Elk threw his knee into my stomach. I rolled back. He stood and ran forward to pounce on me. With a kick, I swept him off his feet. I stood before he could regain his balance. With a cry, I threw my body on his. I heard muffled words as he fought to get loose from the hold. Suddenly, I swung to his chest, pinning his shoulders in the snow.

A vessel bulged on Little Elk's forehead as he struggled to get free.

At last, Chief Long Bow came and stood over us. He looked down, a slight smile pulling at the corners of his lips. He said words in Pawnee and the Indians cheered.

Chief Long Bow squeezed my shoulder and motioned for me to release Little Elk. I stood, and as I did, more cheers went up for me.

Little Elk lay in the snow defeated, his eyes blazing a hot hatred.

A brave called Big Knife walked over and handed me the locket lost in the snow during the fight. Looking up, I saw the proud expression on my adopted father's face.

###

On horseback, we continued toward the village. The snow continued throughout the days and nights in large, fluffy flakes. I looked back at the long line of mounted braves. They were hunched mounds of cold whiteness in their buffalo blankets. They rode slowly dipping down one ravine and climbing up another.

Chief Long Bow, after the brief squeeze on the shoulder and the proud glance, never looked directly at me again. It was obvious he wanted to show no favortism.

Big Knife, the Indian youth who returned the locket to me, was friendly. At night we bedded down close to one another. Even though we didn't understand one word the other said, we still communicated with gestures and smiles.

For three days we traveled. I knew every step the pinto took brought me further from civilization and the white man. I yearned to hear just one word of English.

Early, the morning of the fourth day, we paused and looked down from a snow-covered summit. Far into the misty distance there was an indistinct outline of a village. People and animals moved about. A shiver of dread ran through me.

Dozens of skinny, barking dogs ran from the village to greet us. I looked down at the poor animals and my heart dropped. They snapped and nipped at the horses' legs looking more wild than tame. Morning fires produced smoke circling out of smoke holes in roofs.

As we rode into the village, children ran along, looking curiously up at me.

The Indians dismounted and the women came to gather

120

the supplies, blankets, and to tend to the horses. They chanted a shrill, wavering prayer in unison. As I dismounted, people old and young came running. They surrounded me at once and looked at me. Everybody talked at the same time and the noise and confusion hurt my ears.

Chief Long Bow pushed his way through the crowd. He threw his buffalo robe aside and pulled the robe from my shoulders. Gently, he pulled my beaver skin hat from my head. The women, old people, and children gasped as they viewed my blonde shoulder-length hair. Chief Long Bow spoke to them. He clapped me on the back and laid his arm around my shoulders. Everyone cheered and smiled.

My attention was drawn to a girl standing before me. Her eyes were as black and large as walnuts. Her hair swept to the middle of her back straight and raven-winged in color. Her clothing was buckskin with a beaded neck. The length met her rawhide boots reaching up her calves. She smiled and turned shyly away.

Little Elk looked from the girl to me. His eyes squinted suspiciously. He knotted his huge hands into tight balls. I recognized the expression of jealousy.

I was led into Chief Long Bow's house. A blazing fire greeted us as we entered. In moments, I felt warm to the bone for the first time in many days. A bird was roasting over a spit and juices from it sizzled as they struck the flames. A plump, friendly Indian woman knelt beside the fire. She was shy but her smile was warm. This was my foster mother, Gentle Winds.

The woman shook out the buffalo blankets and laid them beside the fire. Chief Long Bow sat on one side and motioned for me to sit on the other. In moments, the woman packed Chief Long Bow's bone pipe. She held a stick in the fire and when it ignited, lit her husband's pipe.

Chief Long Bow passed the pipe to me after he had puffed it a few times. After one draw on the harsh tobacco, I coughed until my face turned red. The woman giggled and Chief Long Bow tossed his head back and laughed. Reaching out, they both laid their hands on my arm.

After we ate the roasted pheasant and a root that tasted very much like a potato, I laid down on the blanket beside the fire. In moments I was asleep. And for the first time in days the stark, belly wrenching fear left me.

I was rousted from my sleep by the woman shaking my shoulder. Opening my eyes, I looked up. My eyes followed a pair of moccasins, a pair of buckskin-clad legs, on up to a thick waist, flat belly, and bull chest. This was topped with huge shoulders and a face covered with a thick bush of dark whiskers.

"Welcome to the village, lad," the man said smiling.

Rubbing my eyes, I sat up. This was the first white man I had seen in many days.

"Don't be afraid, lad. I'm not a vision." He felt his arms. "I'm really here in flesh and bone," he said laughing.

His voice was booming and seemed to shake the walls of the little hut.

"I didn't think I'd ever hear a word of English again," I said. "Who are you? Are you a captive too?"

The man laughed again and sat down beside the fire, his legs crossed before him. "No. No one would dare want to capture Donald Masters. I would eat my captors out of house and home."

I laughed.

"No," he said shaking his head, "I'm just a lowly trapper and fur trader. I visit the Chief and his village twice a year and trade with them."

"You know these people well, then."

"Of course, I do. I'm the only white man most of them have seen not counting you. And I keep my face so covered with whiskers that they don't really see much of my skin."

I scooted closer to the man with interest. "Tell me about them. What are they like? What is it like to live here? Do you think there's any chance of me escaping? Would you help..."

"Whoa, there!" He held up his hand. "Hold on, lad. Not so many questions. I don't even know your name yet."

I blushed with embarrassment. "I'm sorry. My name's Davey Hutchins and I'm a member of the Louisiana Purchase exploration party headed by Captain Lewis and Captain Clark."

The man brushed away his coon skin hat and scratched his head. "Well, I'll be. I've heard about the expedition. Word has been spreading for months. I thought the whole lot of you had been drowned or killed by raiding Indians."

I shook my head. "No, sir. We haven't lost one person yet. We're not far now from our destination...the Pacific Ocean!"

"You say that with real pride, son."

"I am proud, sir."

"You're kind of young to be on such a trip, aren't you, lad?" He fished in his pocket pulling out his pipe. In moments the bowl glowed and a haze circled from it.

"Yes, sir. I suppose I am. I wanted to go in the worst way. I'm from Missouri originally. I help the cook and do odd jobs for the men. My dog Snooker and I have been with them from the start at St. Charles."

"Your dog? Where's the dog now?"

"Chief Long Bow wouldn't allow me to bring him. He wanted to leave everything that would remind me of the white man's ways."

He shook his head. "Probably just as well that you didn't. You see, the Indians don't really use dogs as pets too much. They let them forage for themselves and they get real wild. Besides, they eat many of them in the winter. More than likely they would have banned together and fought your dog until they killed him. It's lucky he stayed behind."

I had heard about tribes eating dogs. "Snooker has single handedly battled a grizzly. A bunch of dogs wouldn't have scared him." Secretly, I was happy he did stay behind.

"Well, I'm right proud to meet you, Davey Hutchins. And I'm especially proud to meet such an honorable member of the famed Lewis and Clark expedition." He stuck out his hand.

I reached for his hand, wincing at the bear-like strength of it.

"So, Chief Long Bow took you away from the expedition. He adopted you as his son, I hear. A sad day it was when he lost Running Bear in a battle with the Sioux. His heart and soul was in that boy. He taught him how to ride and hunt. I never knew a man who missed his son so much."

"It still isn't right for him to take me away from my people," I said angrily.

Masters nodded. "Right you are, of course. But, perhaps it's not right for your expedition to come into these peoples' land and intrude on them."

I looked sadly away. "That's what Teddy, the cook, said. Even though we bought the territory from France, maybe we still have no right here. After all, these people have lived here for hundreds of years."

"That's true. But, I suppose that's how governments work and always will. The United States has to do what it thinks is its destiny."

I whispered. "I still want to get away. The trouble is, even if I were to get away, I don't think I could find the expedition again." A shiver ran through me. "I might as well decide to make the best of it."

Masters smoked his pipe thoughtfully. "That's probably the best. Chief Long Bow is a proud man. He would go after you. If I helped you, it might be my scalp. And besides, I would lose their friendship, and the friendship and trust of all the other tribes around here." Reaching out, he squeezed my shoulder. "I hope you understand my position, Davey."

I nodded. "Yes, sir. I understand."

"Good. And now," he said with a big grin, "pass me a big chunk of that roasted bird. I'm so hungry I could start chewing on my moccasins."

Looking up, I burst out with laughter.

Chapter 18

Life with the Pawnees was hard in the winter. As the snows continued, food became increasingly scarce. Hunting parties went out and spent days looking for game. They finally returned empty handed or with one or two jays and a half-starved squirrel. The meals Gentle Winds prepared were more and more meager. Still, she made do with what she had. She always mixed spicy herbs and roots together with whatever meat was available and came out with a delicious stew. And there still was some smoked fish and pemmican left.

I noticed the dog population was getting smaller each day. I shivered thinking how close I came to bringing Snooker with me.

My friendship with Donald Masters grew. The big trader had to stay in the village for a time and wait until the weather improved. We talked by the hours at night around the campfire about the expedition, farming back in Missouri, and the city of St. Louis. He had very little schooling but knew nature and survival in the wilderness better than anyone. I knew he was leaving soon. All contact with the white man's world would be over then.

At night, on my buffalo blanket beside the glowing embers of the campfire, I took Prissy's locket out and looked at her picture in the shadowed darkness. It startled me to realize I had not seen her in fifteen months. Perhaps she had forgotten me, I thought. Perhaps, it would be better if she did. I slept restlessly that night.

Chief Long Bow had hunted with me for weeks until I

became skilled with the bow and arrow. This was my first hunt alone. Carefully, I tracked a lone buck for hours.

Dismounting, I looked closely at the glazed snow. The deer's hoofprints were easy to see. Bringing an arrow out of the quiver, I fitted it into the bow.

I thought about the pride in Long Bow's eyes when I hit the target, won a wrestling match, ran the fastest, or rode my pony more skillfully than any brave in the village. I remembered pa's look of pride when I accomplished something on the farm. They both had the same look in their eyes. But, the thought of escape was with me night and day.

My breath caught. A ten-point buck pawed at the snow to reach some moss not ten yards from me. I waited, not chancing the almost silent approach of my moccasins in the snow. It was majestic, and strength rippled through its body. I always felt a little sad when something so beautiful had to die. I knew the village was in serious need of food. I heard stories about the winter's food being so scarce the Indians had to eat bark off of trees to keep from starving to death.

The buck raised its head, sniffing the air. I waited, holding my breath, until the animal turned to just the right position. It looked away as I drew back the sinew string. Pausing, I aimed carefully. The arrow sung through the cold air, finding its target. The buck reared up on its hind legs and started forward. Suddenly, it lurched back and fell to its side. I ran forward to be sure it was dead. I didn't want the grand beast to suffer one moment.

Looking up, I saw movement next to the stream. I inserted another arrow into the bow. It was Yellow Flower, the Indian girl I had met the first day I arrived in the village. She was kneeling beside the stream filling a pot with water.

I motioned toward the buck. "Look! Look, Yellow Flower. I got a deer for the village. There will be meat for everyone tonight!"

128

Yellow Flower looked up and smiled. Getting to her feet, she followed me to the deer. Her eyes settled on the beast laying in the snow. Her hand examined the sure arrow which had found its target so accurately.

She smiled and said a few words in Pawnee. I understood two of them..."mighty hunter".

Walking up to her, I noticed how her hair shone in the morning sunlight. I looked around. A purple mountain flower poked through a mound of snow. I raced to it and picked it. Shyly, I handed it to her.

A bolt of pain struck the side of my head. I wavered for a moment and then dropped to the snow. Looking up through blurry vision, I saw Little Elk sneering down at me. Just before my head fell back into a pit of blackness, Little Elk grabbed Yellow Flower's hand and pulled her toward his horse tied in the distance.

After a time I awoke from the blackness. Blood ebbed slowly down the side of my head. Pushing myself to my feet, I stumbled forward.

I searched the surrounding area seeing the red smudge of blood in the snow where the buck went down. The animal was gone. I was sure Little Elk had taken Yellow Flower and my buck back to the village.

Gentle Winds' hands moved carefully along the cut. She removed the blood and dirt and placed a clean cloth around my head. Masters told Gentle Winds and Long Bow what I had told him: I had slipped on some ice while hunting and hit my head on a rock.

Outside, next to the ceremonial building, the large buck was rotating over a pit of hot coals. There was a celebration of singing and dancing. Drums beat and reed whistles were blown. Everyone was happy that their bellies would be filled again. Little Elk sat in a place of honor on the buffalo blanket. He had brought home the prized buck and fooled the evil spirit of starvation away.

I sat in the hut refusing to go out and join the happy crowd.

Big Knife entered the hut and knelt beside me. He always wore an open smile. Big Knife was not one of the most skilled horsemen nor did his arrow find the target very often, but he was a good friend.

He set a plate of choice pieces of venison before me. I shook my head refusing to eat it. He looked confused.

Donald Masters came into the room. His large frame cast a huge looming shadow on the walls.

He examined Gentle Winds' bandage. "It looks as though your ma has taken good care of you."

I bit into my lip, not liking him to refer to Gentle Winds as my ma.

"A strong lad like yourself will mend fast, Davey. Gentle Winds will watch over you."

I nodded but refused to smile.

Masters looked down at the plate of uneaten meat. "You haven't touched the venison. Go ahead; it's delicious. Little Elk has his faults everyone knows that, but it looks as though this time he's done something worthwhile. If his chest puffed up much further it would explode." He laughed.

"When are you leaving, Donald?" I asked. "When are you going on?" I knew I must know the truth, even though I dreaded to hear it.

Masters picked a piece of venison from the plate and poked it between his lips. "My feet are starting to get the itch to travel. I hope this weather lets up soon. If it does, I'll probably be leaving in a week or two."

"Oh," I said sadly. "If you would happen to see anyone in the Lewis and Clark expedition, would you tell them I'm okay and for them not to worry?"

Masters nodded. "I'll do just that, Davey. I'll also get in

touch with your family back in St. Louis if I'm ever there and tell them about you. I know they'll want to know you're safe even though you're living with the Pawnees."

I hung my head. "Yes, be sure and let them know. Maybe...maybe someday..." My voice trailed away in sadness.

Masters reached out pressing my shoulder. "I know how you feel, boy. I would feel the same way. The Pawnees are by and large good people. I figure you will try to escape some day. It's only a matter of time."

"I want to be with my own people." I sighed. "Gentle Winds and Long Bow are good people. My life here is not that bad. It's a hard life that's true, but I'm used to a hard life in the wilderness. There's one thing I've never had to deal with before and that's to worry about having enough to eat. I feel sorry when I see the little kids hurting from hunger. I know Chief Long Bow is sad and hurts because of their pain."

"You're right there, lad. Chief Long Bow has always been a good chief. He wants nothing but the best for his people. When his people are hungry, no one hurts or worries more than he does. You've noticed that he goes out every day to find food, and when he does, he shares it with everyone."

All the time we talked, Big Knife followed our conversation, looking from one to the other. He smiled and nodded when we nodded, shook his head when we shook our head. He hadn't understood one word, but he was happy being in our company.

Suddenly, the dancing and the music stopped outside. Shouting and angry voices were heard. I turned, hearing running feet.

"What's happening out there? Why has the celebration stopped?" I asked.

Masters got to his feet. Just as he leaned to go out to investigate, Chief Long Bow and Yellow Flower came into the hut.

Chief Long Bow stood straight dressed in full ceremonial costume. He motioned for Yellow Flower to be seated. She sat there shaking uncontrollably, looking down at the floor.

Chief Long Bow's eyes were rolling wildly with anger. He looked toward me and pointed to the raw cut on my head. Yellow Flower continued to shiver.

Long Bow talked at length to Masters. Big Knife said nothing, but his eyes darted from the Chief to me and then to Yellow Flower's bowed head.

Chief Long Bow's arms flung toward the ceiling as his anger increased. Gentle Winds came to his side to try to calm him.

Finally, the chief was finished. Masters turned to me.

"Why, Davey?" he asked.

"Why, what?" I replied.

"Why did you try to protect that scoundrel, Little Elk? Yellow Flower told Chief Long Bow the whole story. She told him how you killed the buck. She told him about Little Elk hitting you with the stone and then claiming the kill as his own. Why did you make up the story that you fell on some ice and hurt your head?"

"I didn't see that it made any difference. I didn't want to get Yellow Flower involved. And besides, it would have been my word against his. I don't think a white man's word is worth all that much around here, even if he is the adopted son of the Chief."

Masters turned to Chief Long Bow and relayed my words.

Chief Long Bow looked stern but his eyes remained soft with understanding. At last he nodded and spoke.

Masters listened for a time and then spoke to me. "Davey, the Chief is sorry you felt you could not tell the truth about what happened, but he understands how you feel. He also wants you to come with him and take your rightful place on the buffalo blanket of honor. You deserve it and the honor is rightfully yours."

132

I shook my head.

Masters' voice grew stern. "Davey, don't do this to the Chief. The mighty hunter must take his place of honor at the ceremonies. It is a tribal tradition."

I looked up at Chief Long Bow, seeing the concern in his eyes. At last, I nodded. Chief Long Bow reached out and pressed my shoulder. Yellow Flower looked at the earthen floor of the hut.

Reaching out, I lifted her chin and looked into her enormous black eyes. I smiled and said: "Thank you, Yellow Flower. It took a lot of courage to do what you did."

She nodded with understanding and smiled.

Chief Long Bow placed his arm around my shoulders. The moment we walked out into the cold, dark night, a shout of thanks went up from a hundred people.

I was warm inside. For the first time since coming to the Pawnee village, I felt better. I smiled and waved my hand. Out of the corner of my eye, I caught Little Elk cowering in the darkness, his head bowed in shame.

Chapter 19

Just when the weather looked as though it might calm, another storm hit. The wind howled and the snow piled up blocking the entrances to the huts. There was nothing anyone could do other than huddle close to the campfire in the hut and listen to the mournful wail outside.

People started getting sick. At night I covered my ears to block out the pitiful coughing of people in the village. Gentle Winds boiled roots in a broth. There were no dogs left. I couldn't get over the strange quietness due to the absence of barking. Some of the people started peeling bark from trees and digging through great depths of snow for roots of any kind. A muskrat, field mouse, or marten was hastily skinned, boiled, and eaten eagerly.

Donald Masters stayed with the Indians. The severe weather demanded it. His skin hung loosely on his huge frame.

The strong braves stumbled with weakness. Yellow Flower's large eyes looked even bigger set in her gaunt face.

While being prisoner in the hut during the long storm, Donald Masters taught Chief Long Bow a few English words and also taught me some words in Pawnee.

One morning Chief Long Bow reached over to me and pressed my shoulder. There was a big smile on his face. "You...my...son..." he said in a halting voice.

Still, I could not call him my father.

Chief Long Bow smoked his bone pipe with the harsh tobacco.

Donald Masters came into the hut. He beat the snow from his coonskin hat and brushed off his bearskin coat. He sat down crosslegged and took out his pipe. He puffed on it contentedly for a few minutes.

After he was settled, Chief Long Bow spoke to him. Masters quickly glanced toward me and turned back to the Chief.

Finally, Masters cleared his throat. "Davey, the Chief thinks it's time he told you a little bit about his son....the son you replaced."

Chief Long Bow spoke quietly in his native tongue. Gentle Winds was sitting in the darkness, her head bent with sadness.

After a time Masters turned to me. "The Chief wants you to know something about his son, Running Bear. He asks you to listen."

I looked toward the Chief and nodded.

Masters continued. "Chief Long Bow said that Running Bear was a son like no other. He could run the swiftest, ride the best, was the most accurate marksman, and beat everyone in wrestling. And yet he was not one bit bloated with pride. He cared for every living thing from human being, to animal, to plant. He was strong as an oak but as gentle as a spring blossom. He was filled with life. He laughed readily and cried easily when someone hurt. He had a perfect balance of tenderness, courage, and strength." Masters looked up at Chief Long Bow and noticed his eyes fastened on me. "The Chief said that when his son was killed, his own soul was pulled out of him and wandered without purpose for many months. He could not hunt. He could not sleep. He could not eat. He wandered through the mountains looking for his soul and the soul of his dead son. The nights were endless and the days were bleak. His son would have taken his place as Chief of the Pawnee nation and he would have been the greatest chief ever. He would have wed the lovely Indian maiden, Yellow Flower, and they would have had beautiful, courageous, and gentle offspring." Masters looked at me. "And now he has you as a son. He said that he knew when he saw you in the white man's camp that you were

136

not ordinary. You reminded him at once of his dead son, Running Bear. He feels ashamed he had to bring you here as a captive, but his grief over the loss of Running Bear made him do it. He knows you will be an equally good chief when the time comes. Your strength, courage, skill and yellow hair will make you famous throughout all Indian nations. You are riding Running Bear's prized pinto pony. And one day you will marry the maiden that Running Bear was intended to marry, the lovely Yellow Flower."

I gulped and looked at Masters and back again to the Chief. "Marry!" I said with disbelief. "Yellow Flower is a wonderful girl, but I could never marry her. She is very young yet." I jabbed my chest with my thumb. "I'm too young to get married."

Masters grinned mischievously. "Indians get married very young. You and Yellow Flower will be just about the right ages in about two years." He pursed his lips and closed his eyes in thought. "Yes, I think that would be about right." He reached out and slapped me on the back. "You'd make a great husband in about two years, Davey, lad."

I glanced into the corner and saw Gentle Winds with a wide grin on her face.

Donald Masters laid his head back and laughed. Chief Long Bow and Gentle Winds followed. I thought it must sound strange to the rest of the village to hear this chorus of laughter leaking through the howling storm in the half-starved Pawnee village.

Days passed and the blinding snow continued. The Pawnee people peeked out of their huts each morning hoping that the overcast sky had cleared. They prayed to their gods to stop this unending storm. No one left their fireside unless it was to go for more wood or to scrounge for morsels of food. Old people and children became sick. They lay on buffalo blankets, their eyes large and glazed from lack of food.

People waded waist-deep in snow when they left their huts. Gentle Winds sat hunched and unsmiling beside the fire. A buffalo blanket lay across her shoulders.

Long Bow's dark face was etched in pain. No one had returned with game in many days.

On the morning Gentle Winds was too weak to rise from her bed, I saw the flicker of decision flash in Long Bow's eyes.

I sat saying nothing as the Chief strapped snow shoes to his feet. He rose and walked out without looking back. He trudged to Yellow Flower's hut to bring her back to look after Gentle Winds while he was gone. I was tense as I stocked my quiver with sharpened arrows and packed a few hard, stiff strips of pemmican.

"I'm going with Long Bow, Gentle Winds," I said kneeling down looking into her dull eyes.

Gentle Winds said nothing but nodded.

"I want you to get well while we're gone. Let Yellow Flower nurse you back to health."

Long Bow strode into the hut. Yellow Flower followed timidly behind him. Her eyes found me in the shadowed darkness of the lurching flames.

Donald Masters bolted through the door. His huge bear skin coat hung on his skeleton-like frame. He started to cough and his face turned a deep red.

The big man smiled and clapped me on the shoulder. "Well, Davey, it looks like you and the Chief are about ready to strike out." His face grew serious. "Be careful. I don't see any signs of it letting up. A man could freeze to death out there."

Chief Long Bow talked to Masters for a time. At last Masters turned to me.

"The Chief says that it is better to die trying to save his

people than to waste away in a warm hut. He says he is proud of you for going with him."

"Tell the Chief that I want to go. I am proud to go on the hunt with him."

Tears banked in Masters' eyes. He brushed the wetness away with the back of his gloved hand and told the Chief what I had said.

A proud smile came to Chief Long Bow's face. He went to the back of the hut and brought out a new pair of snow shoes he had made just in case I decided to go.

Masters coughed. "I wish I could go with both of you. I'm afraid I'd only slow you down. I don't think I'd make it a hundred yards through that snow."

I nodded. "The Chief and I understand, Donald. We both want you to stay here and look after things." I looked down at the sleeping woman and frowned.

"I'll do just that Davey, lad. I'll stay and see that things go smooth-like." He glanced over at Yellow Flower who was already making an herbal broth for Gentle Winds over the campfire. Masters smiled. "And I'll look after that pretty wife-to-be for you, lad."

My face flushed and I looked away. "There's time to talk about that when we get back," I said with a disgruntled tone in my voice.

Chief Long Bow returned to the serious matter at hand and checked our supplies. We had quivers filled with sharp bone-tipped arrows. We had plenty of flint for fires. We had a small stock of pemmican to maintain our strength. We had snow shoes, warm buffalo blankets and robes. Our hands and heads were covered with skins. He nodded his approval.

Chief Long Bow knelt and looked at Gentle Winds. He said a few words in Pawnee and brushed her hair from her forehead. Finally, the Chief turned and shook Masters' hand. Quickly, he left carrying his snow shoes.

I clasped Donald Masters' hand and started to walk

out of the hut. I stopped and looked back over my shoulder. I saw through her tear-brimmed eyes Yellow Flower was bidding me goodbye and a safe return.

Chapter 20

The wind blew across our faces, lashing us with its might. As far as we could see, there was an unending layer of whiteness on the earth. The mountains stood solidly in inverted, jagged cones.

Chief Long Bow led the way. He walked with long, strong strides even though it had been days since he'd eaten. Now and then he stopped to check my progress. When we stood on a knoll or ledge our eyes scanned the land below looking for any beast venturing out in the storm to feed.

We stopped to drink from icy mountain streams and to chew on tough strips of pemmican. Carefully, we measured the meat never knowing how long it would have to last.

For three days we trudged through the wilderness looking for signs of game. We had yet to shoot one arrow. At night we huddled close to the fire, our bellies screaming with hunger.

I dreamed of Aunt Maude's declicious table. I saw visions of fried ham, sourdough biscuits, homemade plum jelly, apple pies and cinnamon rolls. My mouth watered and I would awaken hungrier than ever.

On the fourth day the pemmican was gone. On the fifth day we stood on a rocky knoll and looked at the land below. Chief Long Bow pointed. An excited smile parted his lips. Below, a huge elk pawed trying to swipe the snow away to reach some covered vegetation. His antlers were wide and stately. Already, I imagined how many bellies it could feed back in the village.

At last the snow ceased and the sky was clear. The sun leaked out from behind a fluffy barricade of clouds.

Perhaps the prayers of the Indian gods were starting to take effect, I thought.

Chief Long Bow started forward. His foot slipped on a rock jutting from a mound of snow and he fell. I watched him fall from the ledge and hit thirty feet below. He continued rolling head over heels down the slope. A spray of snow trailed the tangle of arms and legs.

The elk looked curiously around without alarm. Suddenly, it bolted and leaped through the snow.

Helplessly, I saw the elk struggle through the snow to escape.

I ran down the slope as fast as I could in the clumsy snow shoes, my heart pounding in my chest. The Chief started to moan.

"Can you move your arms?" I asked, gesturing.

Long Bow understood and moved his arms without pain.

"Now, can you move your legs?" I pointed at his legs.

Chief Long Bow looked down at his right leg and winced. He gasped and his head rolled to one side.

I examined the leg; it was broken at the ankle. Looking up, I saw the sun was already falling and night would soon be setting in. The temperature in the mountains drops quickly when the sun goes down. I knew I had to build him some protection and keep him as warm as possible.

First of all, I braced his ankle on both sides with pieces of wood binding them together with strips of rawhide. "You're going to be all right," I said. "I'm going to build a lean-to to protect you from the cold and wind." I motioned toward the trees. "And then I'm going to build a fire so we can keep warm during the night."

Chief Long Bow said words in Pawnee. I nodded and hurried to get the lean-to and fire ready before the cold night shrouded over us.

Even though the wind increased and the temperature

fell, I sweated beneath my buffalo skin clothing. I tore pine boughs from the trees and soon had a warm protection for the Chief. I placed Chief Long Bow beneath it and hollowed out the snow so even that would give him protection from the wind. Next, I used the flint to start a fire. Soon a fire was crackling and flames lurched into the blackness. I found a running mountain stream close by and filled a buffalo bladder with water. Chief Long Bow drank eagerly. I wished I could find something to eat to calm the rage of hunger in both our bellies. Chief Long Bow fell asleep amid painful groans. I sat close by on my buffalo blanket staring into the black mountain night.

I wanted to stay awake and guard the Chief while he slept but I knew I must have sleep if I were to be able to have the strength to do anything to help our survival.

Shuffling the embers of the fire, I threw on more dried wood. The worst thing possible would be for the fire to go out. A strong fire was good protection and was needed to keep us from freezing to death.

"Maybe I could just rest for awhile," I said drowsily. "I"ve got to get some sleep or I'll never be able to handle tomorrow. I've got to figure a way to get the Chief back to the village." My voice trailed off as I lowered my head to the buffalo blanket and fell asleep.

###

I slept soundly for hours. I shivered feeling cold to the marrow of my bones. My eyelids opened slightly checking the fire. Nudging the blanket back, I looked at the dying fire with its dull glow. I shuddered. I started to pull the blanket back over my eyes when I saw a shadow sweep past me in the moonlight.

With stiff fingers, I pulled the blanket back further and peered beyond the fading light of the fire. There was movement out there; I was sure of it. I listened carefully.

My ears picked up the brittle sound of sparks crackling in the fire. I heard the wind in the trees. But, there was something else, I told myself. There was a sound that I couldn't identify. It sounded like breathing or perhaps panting.

Stirring the fire, a lazy flame darted from beneath an uncharred piece of wood and licked at the night.

I saw them then. Their eyes gleamed in the firelight. I looked at the sides and behind me. They were everywhere. We were completely surrounded by large, hungry timber wolves! My heart thundered in my chest.

Looking around at the Chief, I knew I had to warn him of the danger.

"Chief Long Bow! Wake up!" I shouted.

The pack lurched back, hesitated, and came forward again.

Chief Long Bow opened his eyes. Painfully, he sat up and looked around in disbelief.

Getting to my feet, I put an arrow in my bow ready for any attack.

Chief Long Bow took a limb in his hand after realizing he had lost his bow and quiver of arrows in the fall.

The wolves, gaunt with jutting rib cages, walked slowly in a circle. I pivoted, keeping my eyes on every one of them.

The band of wolves waited patiently. They knew we were outnumbered. There was no hurry.

In the dim firelight I saw the drool seep from the corners of their mouths and drop to the snow. Their razor sharp fangs glinted in the blood-red gums. Their ears lay back and the hair on their necks bristled. I wished Snooker were here right now, I thought.

"We'll take care of them. Don't worry," I said. "I'll kill the first one that makes a move forward." I stood poised on the balls of my feet.

Their strong, gamey smell swept over us. They continued to circle. There was already a worn path.

144

Long Bow shouted and waved the club. A couple of wolves lunged back, but after a short retreat came forward.

My mouth was dry. I kept telling myself that if we could hold them off until dawn maybe they'd go away.

One wolf bolted forward and snapped at my leg. I kicked him in the muzzle. The wolf yelped in pain and darted back.

"And there's more of that if you try it again!" I shouted.

Long Bow shouted proudly waving his club.

The wolves walked in a circle, waiting.

Long Bow yelled in pain. I whirled in time to see a huge timber wolf snarl and then bolt forward again and bite into his shoulder. I spun and took little time to aim. Pulling the sinew cord back in one smooth movement, the arrow whistled through the night landing in the wolf's side. The animal howled and ran back to the pack. Once there, it crumpled to the ground and kicked helplessly.

Suddenly, another wolf advanced and tore the leg of my breeches. Picking up a limb, I brought it down with a crash over its head. The animal howled and fell stunned to the snow.

The pack became increasingly restless, smelling our blood and the blood of their fallen members. They advanced two and three at a time. They barked, growled, and snapped at us and then retreated.

"Come on, if you think you can. You'll end up like your brothers over there!" I screamed.

My eyes darted from one beast to another. I stamped my feet and shouted at them. The wolves knew there was nothing we could do.

I yelled as a beast tore my breeches from behind. I struck out hitting it in the flank with a club. It howled and retreated but another wolf took its place. I shuddered seeing two more lining up to join in. I swung the club back and forth hitting one now and then but missing them more times than not. My chest heaved with exhaustion.

One wolf rushed forward hitting me at the knees, catapulting me backward. I landed with a grunt on my back. My arrows scattered in the snow. I looked down and winced, noticing the sinew bow string had snapped. Now I had only a club.

Long Bow shouted and beat at two wolves snapping at his broken leg. He was getting weaker by the moment.

I looked up in dread from the ground, seeing the largest and fiercest wolf in the pack glare at me. Its mouth was wide open and the long teeth flashed in the firelight. It growled and crouched low. My throat tightened as the beast prepared to leap. I brought up the club in weak defense. The beast leaped into the cold night. A sharp howl came from its mouth. I lay there frozen with fear.

In the back of my mind, I heard the Chief shout. I saw the huge beast above me, its mouth open, its razor sharp fangs coming closer. Suddenly, a shocked glaze coated the beast's eyes. It landed solidly on its chest. I thrusted my forearm into its open mouth to keep it away from my face and throat. It rolled to one side with a glazed look of death in its eyes. Another wolf took its place. It leaped and was knocked to one side in mid-air.

Jumping to my feet, I swung the club like a wild person. Another wolf advanced but dropped to the snow several feet in front of me. I looked around, confused. I heard the sharp crack of a rifle and another beast crumpled to the snow. The pack retreated when the leader was wounded in the shoulder. They ran together over the snow and disappeared into the night.

I gasped for breath and blinked my eyes as sweat streamed into them. My clothes were torn to shreds. There was a patch of blood on one arm. I glanced quickly to the Chief and found him waving his club assuring me he was alive. How? Why? What? My eyes looked into the blackness.

Suddenly, I stumbled falling on my back in the snow.

There in the shadows of the dancing fire stood the bearded figure of Sergeant Riley.

"Hello, Davey, lad," he said. "I thought I'd start paying you back."

Chapter 21

"Close your mouth, Davey, lad, before you swallow some buffalo gnats," Sergeant Riley said with a huge grin.

Reaching out, I touched his buckskin boots to be sure he was real.

Sergeant Riley laughed huskily. "I'm real all right, Davey. You don't have to worry about that. Your yells brought me running." He gestured with his arms outstretched. "And all of those furry mounds laying there are real wolves who were preparing to have you for supper."

I gulped. "But...but how? How did you find me? I thought the whole party must have reached the Pacific Ocean by now."

Sergeant Riley put out his hand. "Shake my hand, Davey, lad. Shake the hand of a man who's traveled for weeks trying to find you. I stayed hidden when they left our camp weeks ago and followed you for awhile, but I lost the trail. I've been searching ever since."

I grinned and threw my arms around the testy, old soldier. "I can't tell you how glad I am to see you, Sergeant. I was just about eaten alive."

Sergeant Riley shook his head. "You're too tough, boy. They want something tender. They don't want a boy who's been toughened by Sergeant Rasmus J. Riley. Your hide would break their teeth." He laughed and I joined him.

I looked around at the furry humps of flesh laying in the snow. "Did you ever eat wolf meat, Sergeant?"

"I tried it years ago, and even if it's far from roast beef, it's still nourishing. Besides, I really peppered those wolves' behinds with the rifle didn't I, boy?" he asked proudly.

"You sure did. If you hadn't come along when you did, the Chief and I would both be bones by now."

Sergeant Riley looked suspiciously over his shoulder. "What? What are you talking about? Chief? You mean you ain't tryin' to escape?"

"No. Chief Long Bow is lying over there beneath the lean-to. He's got a broken ankle."

Sergeant Riley lifted his rifle and looked warily toward the lean-to.

I pushed the barrel of the rifle away. "Don't worry, Sergeant. He can't get up."

"He's still an Indian, boy. I'm not taking any chances."

"You don't understgand."

"What do you mean I don't understand? That man lyin' over there is the Indian who captured you weeks ago."

I shook my head.

Sergeant Riley stared at the Chief. Their eyes locked in the dim firelight with distrust. "I don't know what happened, Davey, but this isn't right."

"We'll talk about it later, Sergeant. We've got to check the Chief's wounds."

Sergeant Riley jammed his thumb in his chest. "You want me to tend to an Indian?" he asked. "Not on your life."

Hurrying over to Long Bow, I tore the sleeve back and looked at the raw wound on his shoulder. I heated water and washed the wound thoroughly and then bandaged it with a cloth torn from my shirt.

Chief Long Bow extended his hand toward Sergeant Riley in a gesture of gratitude and friendliness.

"He wants you to take his hand. He is grateful to you for saving us from the wolves."

At last Sergeant Riley laid his rifle down out of Long Bow's reach and clasped his hand. "You're...you're welcome...I guess," he said hesitantly.

Sergeant Riley shook his head in confusion. "I'd better get to skinning those wolves so we have something to eat. I've got to put a little meat on that rack of bones. I swear, a good breeze could come up and sweep you away."

"There hasn't been much food in the village for weeks," I said jabbing the fire.

Sergeant Riley was already in the process of skinning the first wolf. One eye was cautiously watching Chief Long Bow in the distance. "Are you saying that things have been real bad for you, lad?" he asked.

I nodded. "It's been bad for all the people in the village. The Chief and I made this last try to get some game because so many people were getting sick."

"Well, we'll be back in camp in a few days. All of this will be behind you. Someday it'll all seem like a bad dream."

Blood from the meat dripped into the fire and sizzled hitting the flames. My mouth drooled smelling the charred meat. I couldn't think of anything except the cry in my belly.

"I don't know any more, Sergeant. It's hard to explain. So much has changed since that day months ago when I left with Chief Long Bow and the Pawnee braves."

Sergeant Riley nodded his head slicing at the wolf's belly. "Yes, but it's over. Tomorrow we'll strike out for the Lewis and Clark camp. We've been stalled up river for weeks because of the bad weather. They promised me when I left they'd wait until the weather broke."

I tore some of the meat from the simmering chunk of flesh and brought it to Long Bow. He swallowed it only half chewed. At last, he groaned in comfort.

I walked back to the fire and roasted another piece. I knew I could say nothing more until I had eaten. The piece of meat still dripped blood when I tore it to bits and gobbled it down. The meat had a wild, rangy taste, but right then it tasted as delicious as turkey and stuffing on Thanksgiving Day to me.

I ate without saying a word for several minutes. Finally, I wiped my mouth with my torn sleeve. "That was the best-tasting meat ever," I said. "I feel my strength coming back already."

151

Sergeant Riley grinned. "That's good, Davey," he said. That's real good."

I looked up through the flames at the bushy-bearded man. "Well, we're even now, Sergeant. You saved my life when you kept the wolves away from me. And you kept me from starving to death when you killed them as well."

Sergeant Riley gestured. "We'll start out before dawn and be on our way. Captain Clark's horse is tied in that grove of trees."

I looked up, still gnawing the bone of the wolf's hind leg. "I can't start back tomorrow or maybe never for that matter," I said.

"What are you talking about, boy?"

"I mean I've got to get the Chief back to the village."

"What? Are you crazy? You can't take that Indian back to his village."

"And why not?" I asked.

"I'd think that would be as plain as the nose on your face. The moment you step foot back in that village you're a captive again. Now is the best chance you'll ever have for getting away from them."

"Are you saying I should leave the Chief here and go back with you tomorrow?"

Sergeant Riley nodded. "Of course. The Chief couldn't warn anyone with that broken ankle."

I jumped to my feet, my hands balled into tight fists. "No! I've got to get him back to the village. He would freeze to death out here. Or worse yet, the wolves could come back."

Sergeant Riley put out his hands in explanation. "But, don't you see, you'll be right back where you started. The minute you get him back things will be just the way they were. You'll be a captive and the adopted son of Chief Long Bow again."

I shook my head thoughtfully.

"I don't like the thought of leaving a man out here to

fend for himself. But, it's our only way to escape. It'll buy us just enough time to get away clean."

"But, he will be dead when they find him...if they ever do."

"The Chief didn't care that much about you when he took you captive, lad. Walking back into that village will be like walking back to being an Indian. You'll have to forget the white man's world forever." Sergeant Riley said in a graveled voice.

I looked away. "I'll have to take that chance. And if you don't want to go with me, I understand. You can go on back to the expedition alone in the morning. And I hope you all make it to the Pacific Ocean."

Sergeant Riley looked at me and shook his head. "You're more stubborn than a barnyard full of mules, Davey Hutchins. I'm as crazy as you are, but if you think I'm walking away from here when dawn comes and let you slip through my fingers after freezing my behind for weeks, you're plumb loco. If you go back to the Pawnee village, I go, too. And that's an order!"

Chapter 22

It was like a miracle. Just when I thought there was no hope, everything got better. Chief Long Bow, Sergeant Riley, and I slept without stirring until the sun woke us the next morning.

I felt refreshed and strong after eating the wolf meat. Sergeant Riley busied himself constructing a travois to transport Long Bow.

The entire morning was busy with preparations to return to the village. The six wolves were tied together and hoisted atop Captain Clark's handsome roan.

I filled a buffalo bladder with water and slung it across the horse. Smiling, I looked at the stream seeing distinct signs that the bad weather was breaking. Mountain flowers poked from the snow.

We broke camp and the roan pulled Long Bow on the travois through the deep snow. Sergeant Riley led and I walked behind. Wolf carcasses dangled from the horse's side. Slowly, we made our way back toward the starving Pawnees.

Our luck continued to improve. One day from the camp, we spotted a deer nudging the snow to get at some grass. Sergeant Riley downed the buck with one accurate shot.

Three days from camp we killed a small elk. The animals were coming back out from their winter protection.

On the fifth day we stood on a rise and looked down at the Pawnee village in the far distance. We saw hazy wisps of smoke curl from the huts. After three hours, we saw people struggling eagerly through the snow. I smiled and waved. I could hardly wait to see Donald Masters, Gentle Winds, Big Knife, and Yellow Flower.

The people cheered recognizing the mounds of meat on

the horse's back. They, too, had killed some game but not enough to quell the firey knife of hunger in their bellies.

Sergeant Riley spat in the snow showing his disgust. The braves chattered excitedly pulling the meat from the horse carrying it triumphantly the rest of the way to the village. Everyone was laughing and talking.

The entire village grouped around us jumping up and down cheering. We were heroes to the people. Even Little Elk cheered.

Donald Masters pushed into the center of the crowd. He shook Chief Long Bow's hand and embraced me.

Chief Long Bow was assisted from the travois and helped into his hut.

"It's good to have you back, Davey." Donald Masters said in a booming voice a wide grin parting his bearded face. "We all gave both of you up for lost. The weather has been rotten since you left except for these last few days. We were sure you both had frozen to death."

I shook my head. "No, Donald. We're all right thanks to Sergeant Riley." I motioned in his direction. "He is a member of the Lewis and Clark expedition. He saved Chief Long Bow's and my life in the nick of time. Those wolves were ready to eat us to the bone."

Stepping forward, Donald pulled off his glove and thrust his hand out. "Pleased to meet you, Sergeant. Any friend of Davey's is a friend of mine."

Sergeant Riley frowned. He looked skeptically at the smiling fur trader and gulped. "Pleased to meet you as well, Mr. Masters. How long have you been a captive?"

Donald laughed. "I'm not a captive, Sergeant Riley. I can come or go any time I like. Chief Long Bow and I are like brothers. I have the greatest admiration and respect for the man."

Sergeant Riley looked around at the many brown, smiling faces. "What about coming into our camp and taking Davey back with them against his will?"

"What are you planning on doing, Sergeant, call in a regiment to battle the Pawnees? The closest military installation is over a thousand miles away."

"It's still not right," he mumbled beneath his breath. "It'll never be right no matter what."

Donald Masters clapped Sergeant Riley on the back. "Relax, Sergeant. We'll go in and talk with Chief Long Bow and have a smoke. Later, after the meat has roasted, we'll attend the ceremonies thanking the gods. At last, it looks like winter is over." He winked at me. "Right, Davey, lad?" He gave me a hard nudge with his shoulder.

I lunged back on my snow shoes and teetered to one side for several moments. At last, I fell head first in a snow bank and emerged covered with snow from head to toe. Everyone laughed and clapped their hands joyfully.

Even Sergeant Riley burst out with laughter.

I was happy Gentle Winds had gotten stronger while we were gone. Yellow Flower had taken excellent care of her.

The four of us sat around the crackling fire telling our adventures. Chief Long Bow and Donald Masters smoked on intricately carved buffalo bone pipes. Sergeant Riley puffed a corncob pipe stuck in the corner of his mouth.

Chief Long Bow waited for the fur trader to interpret the English words. Gentle Winds had set his ankle expertly and the pain had subsided. At times he laughed, not waiting for the Pawnee interpretation. I liked hearing the booming sound of his voice once again.

Through the jumping flames and the haze of smoke, I caught sight of the warm, liquid-black eyes of Yellow Flower. Her silent gaze relayed questions; questions without answers at this point.

At last, the drums started beating, proclaiming the beginning of the ceremonies. Chief Long Bow raised his hand. The smile left and his face was etched with strain. Everyone became quiet sensing the importance of what he was about to say. He turned to Donald Masters. He spoke in Pawnee at length. Donald Masters listened and then looked at me, then to Yellow Flower, and then to Gentle Winds.

Sergeant Riley and I waited patiently, watching the Chief gesture and talk in deep, smooth tones. Sergeant Riley hit the pipe on the bottom of his shoe nervously. "What is it, Masters?" Sergeant Riley asked. "Are they planning something evil for us? Those drums sound scary." He turned to me, his face grim. "I told you, lad, that we should have high-tailed it when we had a chance. Now, it may be too late."

"Don't worry," I said. "I trust the Chief."

Donald put up his hand to quiet the Sergeant. "You've got it all wrong, Sergeant Riley. That isn't what the Chief has planned at all."

"What, then?"

Donald looked at me. "Chief Long Bow couldn't be prouder of you than he is this night. You are the sun, earth, stars, and moon to him, he says. He said to tell you that he cares for you with the same strength and depth he cared for Running Bear."

I smiled at Long Bow.

"Chief Long Bow said you risked your life to save his when the wolves attacked." Donald looked at Sergeant Riley. "And to you, Sergeant Riley, the Chief will be eternally grateful, not only for saving his life but the lives of the people in the village. You are truly a hero and they will tell the legend of your bravery for many years to come."

Sergeant Riley pulled at his beard and blushed.

"He says your bravery has equalled or bettered some of their greatest heroes of the past such as Great Oak, Crawling Turtle, and Dancing Buffalo. He will make you a Pawnee blood brother at the ceremonies tonight with your permission."

158

Sergeant Riley cleared his throat, thick with emotion. He nodded. "You tell Chief Long Bow that I'd be honored to be his blood brother." He traced a finger along the raw scar he had gotten at the hands of another Indian long ago.

Donald turned back and focused his gaze on me. "Chief Long Bow is happier tonight than he's been for a long time. He thinks that Running Bear's spirit has found a home in you, Davey."

I looked up and nodded. "Tell Chief Long Bow that I would be proud to have Running Bear's spirit in me."

Donald relayed my words to the Chief. Chief Long Bow smiled warmly and looked over to Gentle Winds.

I saw a faraway glaze in her eyes.

Donald looked at me once more. "Chief Long Bow wants these ceremonies tonight to be very special for you, Davey. These ceremonies are thanking the gods, Sergeant Riley, and you for all you've done." He paused and licked his lips nervously. "But, they are also the ceremonies to bid you farewell."

My mouth dropped open.

Donald continued. "The Chief talked with Gentle Winds before you came into the hut. They both decided that you should have your freedom and return to your people. Their hearts will break into a million pieces like a clay bowl when you depart. But you are a white boy and you must live in a white man's world."

I was too choked to speak and only nodded.

Donald continued. "The Chief said that you may leave whenever you want. They will be sure you have strong horses and plenty of supplies for the trip back to the expedition. He and Gentle Winds will always think of you as their white son. For now they know that the gods have been truly good to them. The gods have given them two brave sons."

Slowly, I got to my feet and walked over to Chief Long Bow. The Chief put out his hand. I shook it warmly. The drums beat louder beckoning us to the ceremonies. I looked up and saw Yellow Flower looking back at me. Her lower lip was quivering and her eyes were flooded with tears.

The handsome pinto pony, that I had come to call my own, was packed and pawing restlessly at the ground. On his back were bundles of supplies: meat, pemmican, and cakes baked by Yellow Flower especially for the trip.

The air blew in warm breezes and the snow melted, revealing the green vegetation beneath. In valleys there was a blaze of beauty caused by blooming mountain flowers.

Indian braves made many trips to hunt, always returning with deer, antelope, bear, and smaller animals.

The Pawnee people were restless after being forced to remain in their huts for so long. The children, their bellies now full, ran and jumped with new-found energy. They wrestled and hit at one another playfully. The young braves hunted, repaired their huts, wrestled, talked around the fires relating the legends of yesteryear, and pursued pretty maidens.

Donald Masters made plans to leave the village at the end of the week. He still needed a few days to build up his strength.

I bade my best friend, Big Knife, goodbye. Big Knife presented me with a miniature carving of a horse.

Gentle Winds was especially silent the morning of my departure. She worked without raising her eyes to me. She was busy being sure I had a warm buffalo blanket, a new pair of moccasins, plenty of food, and a variety of herbal medicines. She reminded me of Aunt Maude packing my belongings two nights before I left for St. Charles.

Reaching out, she placed her hand on my cheek. I turned abruptly and left through the door of the hut.

I blinked my eyes trying to adjust them to the bright

morning sun. Sergeant Riley, Chief Long Bow, and Donald Masters stood by the horses waiting for me. Chief Long Bow was supported by a homemade crutch beneath his arm.

I looked at the many brown faces waiting to bid me goodbye. My eyes searched the crowd. There was one person I did not see. Yellow Flower was not there.

"Where is Yellow Flower, Donald?" I asked. "I can't leave without telling her goodbye."

"Yellow Flower is particularly sad, Davey. She thought you and she would one day be married." He gestured. "Suddenly, it was not to come true. She is heartbroken." He pointed into the distance. "She's over there. She made an excuse that water must be brought to the hut."

Turning, I ran toward the stream calling for Yellow Flower. In the distance I saw her bending down, looking into the icy water as it swept passed her.

Slowing my gait, I walked up to her, out of breath. She didn't raise her head until my shadow fell upon her. She looked up and I almost stepped back, noting the empty hurt in her eyes.

Reaching down, I took her arm and gently pulled her to her feet. "Yellow Flower, I've come to tell you goodbye. I want you to know that I leave you and the Pawnee village with a heavy heart."

Yellow Flower smiled, understanding only a few words that I spoke in Pawnee.

"I want you to know that at first when I heard that I had a wife all planned out for me as the future Chief of the Pawnees, I wanted nothing to do with it. But, as I came to know you, I could think of no one I would rather have for a wife than you. Your heart is as large as this mountain towering above us." I gestured and looked up.

I took her hand. "I will never know anyone quite like you. I wish only happiness for you."

Yellow Flower blinked as tears ebbed from her eyes. She smiled through the liquid blur and touched my cheek. "Yellow Hair, may the gods smile upon you forever," she said hesitantly in Pawnee.

I understood and smiled. I turned and rushed back to the horses.

The horses were fully packed. The roan and the pinto stood side by side prancing in place, eager to be on their way.

Donald cleared his throat. "Well, I guess this is it, Davey, lad." Reaching out, he shook my hand. "I didn't think it would turn out this way. I knew I'd be leaving in a while but I sure didn't think you'd be leaving before I would." He tried to laugh.

I nodded. "I know, Donald. You have been a good friend."

Donald shook his head. "You could have made it no matter what. You're that kind of lad. I just happened by at the same time, that's all." He grinned and petted his beard. "Who knows, maybe someday we'll run into each other again. Maybe if I get down to St. Louis I'll stop and look you up. Would that be all right?"

"That would be more than all right."

"By that time, I know it'll be easy to find you. Everyone will know the famous Davey Hutchins of the Lewis and Clark expedition." He laughed.

I laughed as well. "That is, if we get back to the expedition before they pull out to continue up river."

He thrust out his hand once again. "Well, goodbye and may God speed."

"Thank you, Donald. Thank you for everything."

I turned to Chief Long Bow saving this goodbye for last. There were so many things I wanted to tell him. I wanted to tell him that I held no ill feeling about being taken captive. I would never trade this experience for anything. I would always have wonderful memories of the village and of the many special people who would always be a part of me.

162

Instead of saying all of these words and having them translated to Pawnee, I looked up into his sad eyes and said these words in Pawnee: "Chief Long Bow...you...my...father."

Chief Long Bow was visibly moved by the words. He nodded and smiled. "Davey," he said in English, "you...my...son."

The two of us embraced knowing we would never see each other again. Each of us lived in different worlds. Each of us had learned to love and respect one another's worlds and cultures.

At last, I pulled away and mounted the pinto. Sitting high astride my mount, I looked back at the sea of brown faces waving at me. I saw Big Knife, Donald Masters, Chief Long Bow, and Gentle Winds peeking from her doorway. Far in the distance, I saw Yellow Flower waving her last goodbye.

Sergeant Riley nodded that it was time to leave. I reined my horse around and started down the rise and away from the Pawnee village.

Chapter 23

Spring arrived gently. The snow melted and the mountain streams rushed in cascading, silver-colored falls.

At times, the horses slipped, losing their footing on the soggy, moisture-drenched ground. The air intermingled with the fragrances of pine trees and mountain flowers.

Sergeant Riley and I nudged our mounts in the flanks, urging them along. Our hope was to reach the encampment before the party of explorers pulled out and continued upstream toward the goal of reaching the Pacific Ocean.

Red-tailed hawks soared gracefully overhead. Squirrels, chipmunks, field mice, and martens scurried in front of us.

At night, lying beside the campfire, I stared up at the sky speckled with a billion twinkling stars. I thought about my experiences these past months with the Pawnees. It seemed like a dream. When daylight flooded through the green lace of pine needles, I felt an excitement as we neared the camp. This was the world I belonged to, I told myself. But, I knew I would be torn between an Indian world and a white man's world for years to come.

Sergeant Riley pulled back the reins and the roan obeyed. He pointed into the horizon. "Just over the rise and down the valley and we'll be back." He paused and shrugged. "That is, if they're still there. Let's hope they've waited for us, lad."

My heart thundered in my chest. For an hour or more we plodded on. At last, Sergeant Riley vented his eagerness and slapped the roan with a switch. The horse bolted to the crest of the rise. "There!" he shouted. "There they are Davey, lad! The camp is still there!"

Kicking my pony, I galloped forward. I looked down on the tiny camp and the figures moving below.

Waving his beaver skin hat, Sergeant Riley shouted. His loud voice echoed through the foothills. Heads looked up; hands came up to shade eyes. Men rushed out of their tents and started running up the rise. They ran stumbling, falling, climbing the hill to greet us.

I clucked my tongue and the pinto bolted forward. I tore down the hill, mud flying from the pony's charging hooves.

I was pulled from the pony, hugged, and pounded on the back. I was passed from one familiar face to another and given warm, strenuous welcomes. Teddy hugged me tight.

I jumped hearing shrill barks. Snooker hobbled on three legs toward me, his tail wagging out of control. I knelt and grabbed him in my arms, squeezing him tightly and was rewarded with lavish, wet swipes of his tongue.

Corporal Tandy beat me on the back, a wide grin on his whiskerless face.

Captain Lewis grabbed my hand and pumped it, almost wrenching it out of the socket with enthusiasm. "Davey," he exclaimed, "thank the good Lord in heaven you're safe."

"Yes, sir. And we should thank Sergeant Riley as well. If it hadn't been for him, I would never have made it back."

I was thrown into the bear-like embrace of Captain Clark. His face was flushed with happiness. He threw his hat into the air revealing the wild tangle of red hair beneath. "Davey, who would have thought we'd ever see you again. It's great to have you back."

Snooker stretched his neck and licked me beneath the chin and along the throat. I giggled feeling the tickling, damp tongue.

"That's the most life that critter has shown in months,"

Corporal Tandy said. "We could hardly get him to move out of one spot 'til now."

At last, after everyone had greeted me, they all stood back to look at me. I looked at them as well. Their clothes were threadbare and hanging loosely on their bony frames. Beards were long and shaggy and most of them wore their hair to the shoulders. It was easy to tell that they, also, had gone through a savage winter.

"I just want to say that Sergeant Riley is responsible for my return. If it hadn't been for him I would still be an Indian. Much worse than that, I would be a pile of bleached bones being gnawed on by a pack of hungry wolves."

Corporal Tandy shouted and cheered and everyone followed his lead. The old soldier was a real hero and had their respect now more than ever before.

The celebration continued with more joking and welcoming. At last, Captain Lewis, always business-like, raised his hand. "It is my sad duty to take all of you away from this happy occasion. But, we still have a mission to perform. And with Davey back it gives us even more of a will to bring our mission to a successful finish and reach the great Pacific. The winter is over and it is past time to continue. At last, our food stocks have been replenished. We will use the canoes the rest of the way." His brows were furrowed as he looked into each face. "We must break camp and plan to leave at once."

I knew we had arrived just in time. Only a day or two later and we would've been left behind.

The party disembarked in six dugout canoes two days later. As we headed up the Missouri, we passed great thunderous falls. Rain drenched us to the skin for three straight days without let up.

On July 4th we stopped along the bank to celebrate the great national holiday of our country's independence. The last of the whiskey was poured out of the cask. Teddy and I roasted an elk and berries were collected. We ate and toasted one another jubilantly. Cruzatte played his faithful fiddle and the men danced. After only an hour of partying, the clouds formed and exploded. A torrential rain halted our merrymaking.

The trek became increasingly cumbersome. The water ran swift and shallow. In the shallows we pulled and poled. The going was slow and backbreaking but we traveled on.

On August eleventh we came upon an Indian trail. One of the men proudly carried an American flag to tell everyone who we were and why we were there. This trail led us into a high gap in the mountains. When it got dark, Captain Lewis ordered a fire built. He was sure we were being watched by Indians. Around the fire he placed the most comely trinkets we had left: looking glasses, awls, beads, and a couple of bright blankets. All night we waited and watched nervously. Suddenly the rain started again and put out the fire. Unknowingly, we had spent the night in the Great Divide. In the morning, we continued west going sharply down-hill. We soon came to a westward-running river. Captain Clark was pleased at its clear appearance. He knew we were now on the Columbia River.

Three days later we came upon a tribe of Indians called the Shoshones. Sacajewea acted as an interpreter being the only member of the party who had any understanding of their language. She relayed the message to Charbonneau and he translated it into English. As they sat around the council fire smoking, Sacajewea recognized one of the chiefs as her brother. She weeped for joy and ran to him. The brother, however, kept his reserve and failed to return her affection.

The Shoshones were poor people. Their staple food was

roots. Sometimes they brought down an occasional bird. But they could seldom get near enough to elk or deer to kill them with bows and arrows. The tribe never heard of maize. Before our party left we gave the tribe several ears and showed them how to plant them. This generosity helped their diet for many years to come.

The tribe had no metal. The women, especially, were fascinated by the small steel awls with which they could make holes in leather to lace thongs.

Captain Lewis was disappointed that there was no direct westward flowing route to the Pacific. We had to go over the mountains again. And we must go immediately, he told us, as there were already signs of frost on the ground.

The party started out. Teddy, due to his advanced age, struggled up the steep trails in breathless gasps. Sharp rocks slashed our moccasins and cut our feet. The wind was savage. Hunger set in once again as the last of the portable soup was used. We drank bear oil after the meat was gone and ate whatever we could hunt or find: a few pheasants, blue jays, and an occasional wolf.

Later that month, we stumbled into another Indian tribe, the Nez Perces. This tribe had never seen white men before. They were not fearful. The exploring party was so rag-tag and weak that we held them no threat. Instead, the people of the tribe helped us. They fed us and mended our clothing. Before we left, they helped us build new canoes. They chose ponderosa pine and burned out the interiors instead of hacking them away. On October seventh, 1805 we set forth once again.

The trip up the Columbia was very difficult. Our canoes were rocked and buffeted by fierce rapids. Sometimes we had to climb steep banks and carry the canoes around treacherous places. There were times, I was sure, we would never make it to the Pacific.

On November seventh, 1805 there was an unexpected lull in the rain. The fog curled back and far into the dis-

tance we could see the vague panorama of the Pacific Ocean. We cheered and threw our hats in the air with celebration. We had made it!

I hugged Teddy, Sergeant Riley, Captains Lewis and Clark, Corporal Tandy, and even Sacajewea. I picked up the ever-smiling Baptiste and swung him around joyously. Baptiste laughed not at all understanding what the great celebration was about. Cruzatte brought out his fiddle and everyone danced even though it was pouring down rain.

I slopped around on the slippery bank tumbling head-first in the mud. I was coated with mud from chin to forehead, but I didn't care at all. We had made it! We had conquered the wilderness. We were the first white men to ever cross it successfully and log its rivers, valleys, mountains, and passages.

It was raining so hard Corporal Tandy had a hard time hearing me even though I was shouting.

"We made it, Tandy! We really made it," I shouted.

Corporal Tandy laughed and pointed at my mud-covered face. "It's still miles and miles off, Davey. But, you're right," he said grinning, "the worst is over."

"I know. At times I thought we were all goners, but here we are close enough to the great Pacific to see it and smell it!" I shouted, the rain pelting my face.

"We've accomplished our mission," Tandy said thoughtfully. "We have established beyond any doubt that the Northwest Passage does not exist. There is no continuous water route between the Atlantic and the Pacific."

I dropped to my knees and hugged Snooker with delight.

Tonight we would eat well, Teddy decided. Hunters brought in game and Sacajewea dug up wappato, a potato-like root of which we were all very fond.

The party traveled the next morning refreshed by the closeness to the end of our journey. We were still many miles from the Pacific shore. We passed many tribes on our way. Among them: Chinooks, Cathlamahs, Killlamucks, Lucktons, Cookoose, Chilts, Youkones, Necketos, and the Potashees. One tribe would signal to the other tribe as our party traveled upstream. I saw the smoke drifting against the westward sky. Sacajewea was invaluable during this time helping us interpret the signals.

As we reached the huge, gray waters of the Pacific, we discovered a skeleton of a sperm whale 105 feet long. The Indians had already stripped away the meat and blubber. The skeleton was too large to send to the President, but we did take careful measurement.

Two days later, we brought down the biggest bird we had ever seen, a California condor. It was nine and a half feet from wing tip to wing tip and three feet, ten and a half inches from point of bill to the tip of its tail.

On Christmas day we passed out the last of the tobacco. The men who did not smoke were given silk handkerchiefs. It was a wonderful occasion.

On New Year's Day we celebrated by dancing with the aid of Cruzatte's fiddle. Indians came from miles around to watch the spectacle. It was now 1806. Winter came once again and we waited impatiently to return down river and home! While waiting, we erected a small fort and called it Fort Clatsop after the Clatsop Indians.

We watched endlessly for a ship, the party was supposed to send, to arrive to give our records, maps, and diaries to. But one never made an appearance. Finally, we packed our supplies, gathered our gear, and wrote many letters and statements. These statements were passed out to certain trusted Indian Chiefs to pass on to any fur traders that happened by. This was in the case the expedition was wiped out on the way back, there would still be a valid recording of our venture and exploration. The journals and scientific material we took back with us. It was March 23, 1806, when the Corps of Discovery shoved off in their tattered canoes toward home.

We were eager to get over the Rockies before another winter set in. Otherwise we would have to stay in the Mandan village while the Missouri was clogged with ice. We jerked and salted as much meat as we could take, most of it deer and elk.

On August 12, we arrived at the Mandan village. I had a warm reunion with my friend, Black Fox. The tribe urged us to stay and they danced and feasted for days. But after the festivities, we replenished our supplies, patched our canoes, and traveled our last leg home.

Charbonneau, Sacajewea, and the papoose, Jean Baptiste, stayed with the Mandan tribe. Captain Clark offered to take the baby back with him to St. Louis and have him educated but his parents thought he was still too young. There was much sorrow leaving Sacajewea and the baby. There was much less for leaving Charbonneau. The man was known to be untrustworthy, lazy, and a bit of a coward. No one shed any tears on his behalf.

As we set off on a south-by-southeasterly course down the Missouri, I turned and waved at Sacajewea and baby Baptiste. My throat was tight remembering the many good and sad times with them. Little did I know at the time what a large part the warm, compassionate Indian woman played in American history and that her name would be known throughout the world.

On down the Missouri, we passed the Sioux. This time, however, the tribe gave us no trouble. There was some name-calling and fist-shaking from the shore but that was all. The party breathed a thankful sigh of relief after passing them.

On Tuesday, September 23, 1806 our tired but proud party paddled into St. Louis, ending a long but very successful trip.

I found out later that a newspaper in Baltimore had learned of us arriving home. It was datelined Baltimore, October 29, 1806. It said: A letter from St. Louis dated

September 23, 1806 announces the arrival of Captains Lewis and Clark from their expedition into the interior. They went clear to the Pacific Ocean. They left the Pacific Ocean on March 23rd 1806 where they arrived on November 1805. The expedition found numerous Indian tribes along the Columbia River which empties into the Pacific. The winter was very mild on the Pacific. The party kept ample journals of their tour which will be published later."

Chapter 24

Closing my eyes, I laid back in the wooden tub. I moaned with contentment at the luxury of my first real bath in over two years. Steam coiled up toward the ceiling of the little room.

Before I climbed into the tub, Teddy cut my hair to a presentable length. Yellow tendrils lay about the floor. I had even lathered my face and swiped away the sparse crop of fuzz growing along my upper lip and under my chin with a straight razor.

Scrubbing myself with a huge sponge, I wrung it out over my head. The itch and discomfort was gone at last. During the months on the trek, I had bathed in mountain streams, rivers, creeks, and took an occasional bath in a wooden tub aboard the keelboat.

I looked down at Snooker dozing peacefully beside the tub. I saw sprigs of gray hair throughout the dark spots on his side. Snooker had aged, I told myself. What a story he could tell if he could speak. He had the scars and wounds of battle to prove it.

Carefully, I reached over the side and swooped him up in my arms, and dunked him beneath the water. Snooker kicked and yiped and splashed water all over the floor.

"You're not going to get out of taking a bath, you old hound. If I'm going to get all spruced up, so are you," I said laughing.

Reaching up, he licked me beneath the chin tasting the suds. His tongue flicked in and out trying to get rid of the bitter lye-soap taste.

I laughed, lathering a cloth and working the soap deep beneath his matted coat.

A soft knock sounded on the closed door.

"Yes, who is it?" I asked.

"It's Teddy, lad. May I come in?"

"Sure, come on in," I replied.

The door swung open and Teddy walked in blinking his eyes trying to adjust them to the steamy room. "Sorry to bother you, Davey," he said. "I just thought we could have a few words while you're getting ready to go see your folks here in St. Louis."

"Sure. Come on in. I'm about finished and as you can see so is Snooker."

Teddy shook his head. "That dog looks as drenched as we were most of the time on the last leg of the trip."

"Well, you weren't. Sacajewea saw to it that you were bone dry," I replied.

The old man sat down on a wooden stool. "Yes, bless that woman's kind heart."

I nodded. "I heard Captain Lewis and Captain Clark talking and they said she would figure very prominently in their reports to the President when they see him."

"Good," Teddy said. "She deserves all the credit in the world. I don't know if we would have made it without her."

I became sad knowing the time was close when I would part company with my friends on the expedition. "What about you, Teddy, now that it's all over?"

Teddy smiled. "Well, as for me, lad, I think it's about time to retire from the army. It's time I hung up my pots and pans." He looked toward the ceiling. "I just want to find a good fishin' hole." He grinned. "Maybe a hole with fish in it as big as the ones we caught when we first started out on the trek. Hauling in those hundred pound catfish was more fun than a barrel of monkeys."

Reaching out, I pressed his shoulder. "The army is losing a good man, Teddy. You'll be hard to replace."

"You ever think about enlisting, Davey? You're a born adventurer and not a bad cook I might say?"

Leaning back, I thought for several moments. "I don't think so. I still think my heart lies on the farm. I like to make things grow. I like the feel and the smell of the soil. I like to be around animals and to work with them. Someday, I'm going to buy a farm. I'll sell my acreage given to me by the government for being part of the expedition. Maybe I'll even be lucky and buy our old farm back."

"That's a good ambition, lad."

"I think my ma and pa would like that. I would never make it in the city. And what would really..." My voice drifted away.

Teddy leaned forward cupping his ear. "What is it, lad? I can't hear you."

"I was just going to say if I could persuade the right girl to come with me, life would look good at this point."

"Are you talking about that pretty miss in the locket?" Teddy asked.

I blushed and pushed myself out of the tub. "Yes, that's the one. Her locket and the memories of her got me through all of it, Teddy." I turned and looked over my shoulder. "I promised her I'd return this locket to her some day. Even when I was being held captive, starving, or the wolves were jumping at my throat, I knew she would help me get through it all."

"You're really taken with that girl, ain't you, lad?"

I started to dress pulling on my breeches. "Yes, I suppose I am."

Teddy threw his head back and laughed. "By jingos, lad, then ask her to go with you someday."

I shook my head. "I don't even know if she remembers me. After all, it's been almost two and a half years since I left St. Louis. A lot could change in that time."

"She'd be pretty dense not to like you. You've proved yourself to be a lot of man during these last few years."

I pulled on my boots and buttoned my shirt. I liked the smell and feel of my new, store-bought clothes. I wiped the steam from a mirror hanging on the wall and brushed my hair.

"What about Captain Lewis and Captain Clark? What are their plans now that it's all over?" I asked.

"I've heard some rumors. Each man who took part in the expedition will be granted 320 acres of public land. Lewis will receive 1,600 acres and Clark 1,000 acres. Both of them are to be promoted to brigadier generals. Lewis is to be appointed governor of the Territory of Louisiana and Clark is to be appointed principal agent for Indian affairs there. Some Indians are already calling him Chief Fire-Hair." Teddy laughed.

"What about Sergeant Riley, Teddy? He hasn't said much about what he'll do."

Teddy scratched beneath his beard thoughtfully. "I heard he'll sell his acreage and remain in the army. I think it'll always be his life."

"Yes, I suppose so. I know I owe him an awful lot."

"He might say the same thing about you, lad," Teddy replied.

"And Corporal Tandy. What are his plans?"

"I've heard him say that he would like to go back into the wilderness and help develop that part of the country. He's young but he's got a lot of spunk and courage," Teddy said wagging his head convincingly.

"Tandy is a real good guy."

"Yes, he is. And as far as the others: some will try to break the soil on their lands and others will sell the acreage and remain in the army." He smiled and looked thoughtfully away. "But, I don't think there's a man who regrets making the trek into the interior."

"That's the way I see it, Teddy," I said. "Everyone came through it all right except for one man we lost from a ruptured appendix."

For a few moments our eyes met. Both of us had shared an experience that few people would ever have the privilege of sharing.

"I can tell you one thing, Teddy. I'm going to miss you

like everything. I'm going to miss your stories and I'm going to miss your biscuits and bear stew."

"I'm going to miss you too, lad. You've been the grandson I've never had." He sniffled and turned his head. "And let me tell you, if you ever need a friend, you can count on Theodore P. Pomroy to be there."

A knock sounded on the hallway door. I looked up.

"I'll get it lad," Teddy said wiping away the wet smudges on his cheeks. "You finish dressing. It's probably the proprietor downstairs coming up to collect his nickel for the bath."

Leaning over, I rubbed Snooker with a towel. He squirmed and barked trying to get free. I laughed and ruffled his fur.

Teddy poked his head around the doorway grinning. "Davey, lad, there's some people out here to see you."

"Is it some of the men coming to tell me goodbye?" I asked.

Teddy's eyes twinkled excitedly. "Why don't you come on out and see for yourself?"

I straightened and walked into the other room raking my fingers through my hair. At the threshold, I stopped and held my breath. Standing there with tears flooding his eyes was Uncle Abner.

At last I smiled and nodded. "I'm home, Uncle Abner. We made it."

With those simple words, I rushed into the big man's open arms. I pressed my face into his broad chest smelling the pipe tobacco. It flooded my brain with memories. I took notice that my head was to his shoulders now.

Uncle Abner pounded my back. "Davey, lad. Thank God you're home safely. We've prayed for you every night since you left that cold, foggy morning from St. Charles."

I stepped back and looked at him. "How did you know we were back?"

Uncle Abner laughed and hit me good-naturedly on the

shoulder. "What do you mean, how did I know? Every American knows about your expedition into the interior. We knew weeks ago you were on the way back. The news of your return is just now racing through St. Louis."

I looked around the room. "You said 'we'. Did Aunt Maude come with you?"

"Do you think I could keep that woman home? She's blamed herself night and day for ever permitting you to go in the first place." He laughed moving out of the doorway.

Aunt Maude stood looking as prim and proper as ever. Her ostrich plumed hat on her head set at just the correct tilt. She gripped a fashionable parasol. The tears in her eyes gave her away. They streamed down her plump cheeks. Her lower lip quivered as she held out her arms and welcomed me into them.

Teddy wiped his eyes at the stirring reunion. Snooker barked excitedly. Uncle Abner stood back allowing his wife the cry she had been waiting for, for over two years.

"The woman will fill two or three buckets before she's through," he said good naturedly.

Aunt Maude ignored him and held me tight. Finally, after several minutes, she forced herself to open her arms. She held a handkerchief beneath her nose and lowered herself to a chair, overcome with happiness and emotion.

I grinned from one ear to the other and introduced Teddy to Uncle Abner and Aunt Maude.

Uncle Abner nodded his head. "You've changed, Davey, lad. You left a boy and returned a man. You're taller, stronger, and probably a whole lot wiser. But, there's still something else about you that I can't quite put my finger on..." He looked at me from the top of my head to the toe of my boots. "It'll come to me, lad. It'll come to me," he said.

"Beg pardon, Mr. Hutchins," Teddy said, smiling. "I think I can tell you what it is. Davey Hutchins has been on one of the greatest ventures known to mankind. He's been tested in every way from near starvation, to being held captive by an Indian tribe, to being almost devoured by timber wolves. He's worked, sweated, learned, and endured. He's measured up in every way. In every way, he's proved himself."

At the mention of near starvation, Indians, and wolves Aunt Maude waved the hanky beneath her nose, fighting the urge to faint.

I shrugged my shoulders with embarrassment. "It's something that will always be with me no matter what happens in the future."

Uncle Abner smiled. "And speaking of your future, Davey. There's someone else waiting to see you. When I said 'we' came to the hotel, I did mean me, your Aunt Maude and..." He paused teasingly until the beautiful, auburn-haired girl took her place in the doorway. "...and Prissy James. She's been counting the hours until she would see you."

Prissy stood in the doorway her eyes brimming with tears of relief and happiness.

I choked and struggled to find words as I always did at the sight of her. Her hair hung about her shoulders in red-gold, cascading waves. Her eyes were just as large and just as blue as I remembered. She too had grown up. She was much closer to being a woman now.

"Davey," she said, her voice wavering. "Davey Hutchins, don't you ever go away again. Do you hear me?" Tears raced down her flushed cheeks.

I shook my head. "I...I won't Prissy. I promise. I won't go more than a few miles from the farm. I promise you." Walking over to her, I dug into my pocket and took out the gold locket. I pressed it in her hand. "Is it okay that I return it to you now in the hotel?"

Prissy looked down into her palm seeing the locket through a veil of tears. "It doesn't matter where or when you return it to me, Davey. What matters is that you're here and you're safe."

182

I opened my arms and Prissy came to me. Tears seeped through her thick lashes.

It was over at last and I was home.

Aunt Maude fanned her handkerchief beneath her nose looking at the both of us. Everyone else smiled and knew that everything had ended just as I had wanted it to.

THE END

Hearth Publishing is immensely proud of Nolan Carlson, their award-winning author, whose dedication to quality literature for the young is unprecedented. Mr. Carlson has been a professional writer for over fifteen years and is the author of six young adult novels. He has served in the public school system as a teacher and school counselor for nineteen years. His books have put smiles on the faces of tens of thousands of people all over the world.

ORDER FORM:

Summer and Shiner, Shiner's Return, Shiner and King, Lewis & Clark & Davey Hutchins

☐ Check enclosed for entire amount payable to Nolan Carlson.

Mail Check to: Nolan Carlson, 4750 Columbian Rd., Wamego, KS 66547

SEND TO:

Name _____

Address _____

City _____

State _____ Zip _____

Phone # _____

	QTY	UNIT PRICE	TOTAL
Summer & Shiner		$6.95	
Shiner's Return		$6.95	
Shiner & King		$6.95	
Lewis & Clark & Davey Hutchins		$6.95	
Shipping and Handling ($3 for first book. Each additional book .50)			
in KS add 6.4% Tax			
		TOTAL	

Wholesale and bookstores: Call Hearth Publishing for orders. 1-800-844-1655

Quantity discounts available.